WHAT THE
HYENA
K N O W S

Other Five Star Titles
by Thomas J. Keevers:

Music Across the Wall

WHAT THE
HYENA
KNOWS

Thomas J. — KEEVERS

Five Star • Waterville, Maine

First Edition
First Printing: December 2005

Published in 2005 in conjunction with
Tekno Books and Ed Gorman.

Set in 11 pt. Plantin.

Printed in the United States on permanent paper.

Library of Congress Cataloging-in-Publication Data

Keevers, Thomas J.
    What the hyena knows / by Thomas J. Keevers—1st ed.
    p. cm.
    ISBN 1-59414-441-9 (hc : alk. paper)
    1. Private investigators—Illinois—Chicago—Fiction.
    2. Photographers—Fiction.   3. Chicago (Ill.)—Fiction.
    4. Texas—Fiction.   5. South Africa—Fiction.   I. Title.
PS3611.E35W43 2005
    813'.6—dc22   2005027044

To Tom, Patrick, Maryellen and Colin, who give new meaning to the old adage, "The child is father to the man." You've taught me more than you know.

ACKNOWLEDGMENTS

Thanks to my old partner, Lt. Jack Lorenz, CPD, for his help in keeping it true.

Thanks to Rae, my life partner, and to Mary Prindiville, for their editorial support.

And special thanks to Art Diers for the gift of so many insights, so subtly provided.

PROLOGUE

It was mid-September, the night I saw the hyena in the park. There was no doubt about what I saw, the moment those savage eyes pierced mine. And even less doubt that I'd tell anyone.

Summer should have been in full retreat by then, but it wouldn't let go, and I had to get out of my stuffy apartment for a while. I drove over to the park, put Stapler on his leash, and headed down one of the asphalt paths. Humboldt Park is supposed to be gang territory, but I never had a problem there. I do carry one of those big mag lights the cops use, just in case the street lamps go out or something. And a snub-nosed .357 Magnum under my shirt.

The air was still, the heat like warm flannel against my face, the glassy surface of the lagoon measled with the reflection of orange street lamps. Lightning pulsed on the eastern horizon like distant artillery. Summer's Invictus.

At the bottom of a hill, the path forked around a low spot filled with rainwater and stinking of dead vegetation. To get away from the smell, I took the fork that led over a little rise, away from the lagoon, past a dark island of trees.

I heard it at first, what sounded like an animal digging in the shrubbery beneath the trees. I stopped; it stopped. I listened, Stapler seeming to take no notice. Then I started to walk on, and a hundred small birds exploded out of the trees, screeching off in every direction. Now Stapler, a bird dog of excellent breeding, went ears forward. A dark form took shape, moved along the base of the trees, separated

7

itself, and drifted across the lighter expanse of grass, angling away from me. Stapler gave a low growl, pressed himself against my leg. I could feel him shivering and I put my hand down to calm him, felt the hair bristling along his back. When the thing was about twenty yards distant, I snapped on the flashlight and, caught in the cone of the bright beam, it whirled, swung its savage head around, round ears cocked, and fixed me with a primitive glare.

Its eyes were like black marbles, opaque, as if they shielded what lay behind, as if all the real light was held inside, and they glowed with knowledge of death and of the night. And with contempt for me—as though I was the intruder exposed in the flashlight's beam, naked in its world.

Then, unhurried, it turned away, loped rump-down across the field and disappeared somewhere on the other side.

I looked around. I was alone. In the distance, an ice cream truck chimed "La Cucaracha." Children were laughing.

I drove home in numb wonder. Where did it come from? How did it get there? When I reached my apartment, I could still feel the chill of those inscrutable eyes, and I turned on all the lights, made myself a drink and sat in my easy chair in the living room.

I knew a hyena when I saw one. As a kid I had been bookish—so much so that my old man, believing I was turning into a wuss, signed me up for the CYO boxing program. He may have been right. Actually, I turned into a pretty good boxer, went to the Golden Gloves a couple of seasons—hell, I coulda been a contendah.

But boxing didn't keep me from books, and especially, in those days before cable TV and the wildlife documentary, books about Darkest Africa. I could identify every single

African mammal. Every ungulate, every predator, every pachyderm. I could tell you what they ate, what ate them. I could name all the antelope in alphabetical order, holding my pals spellbound.

Maybe it was the hyena's very repugnance that fascinated me, but I devoured every word I could find about them, and here is what I know:

Hyenas have both repulsed and fascinated mankind since the beginning of recorded history. Early men thought them supernatural beasts—devil creatures. Pliny the Elder said they were neither male nor female, but hermaphrodites. He had good reason: the female's genitalia look so much like the male's that it takes the palpation of a skilled veterinarian to tell the difference. The clitoris is extended and shaped like the male member, and when she's aroused it grows erect.

Medieval philosophers believed the hyena was not among the animals invited aboard Noah's ark, holding that it wasn't a distinct species at all, but the result of a union between dog and cat. Actually, it doesn't even come close to either species, but is related to the muskalids—weasels and skunks.

It's a mistake to regard them as harmless scavengers, though, the bit players on the African landscape waiting in the wings while lions sate themselves at the kill. True, they are perfectly designed for scavenging, with jaws capable of crushing bones like eggshells. But they also hunt and kill their own food, as solitary animals or in packs.

And they eat humans. They commonly dig up graves near villages, devouring the corpses, but their taste is not limited to the dead. In fact, hyenas are responsible for more human deaths than leopards, especially in the African summer, when natives tend to sleep out in the open. They steal soundlessly into villages in the night, for some reason always seize the slumbering victim by the face, usually taking it off with a single bite. Survivors often say the thing that woke them was the stench of the beast's breath. They drag a victim off and waste not, devouring bones the way we chomp celery. All they leave behind, usually, are a few bits of cloth.

I poured myself another drink, remembering a rash of alien abductions in the news during my college days. I promised myself then that if ever I were taken aboard a space craft by ear-less little men, probed a bit and released, I would never tell anyone. Not my best friend, not the parish priest. No one. Now I was going to bed.

CHAPTER ONE

I was just getting off the elevator, heading for my office, when I heard the sound of a phone resonating along the marble corridor. At the moment I was the only tenant on the floor, and my phone didn't ring that often. I hurried to the frosted glass door, fumbled with the key in the lock, quickly crossed the empty reception area into my office, and snatched it up.

"Legal Investigations, Mike Duncavan." I tried not to sound winded.

"What do you do, sleep at your desk?" It was Stanley Janda, criminal lawyer.

"Stan. I was just seeing a client to the elevator. My receptionist's out sick today." I don't have a receptionist, but Stan's never been to my office. I would have a receptionist, if I had a few more clients, and I hoped Stan was following up on an old promise to send me some business.

"Hey Mike, you remember that time I asked you if you'd stoop to working on a criminal case?"

"Yeah. I said, 'You'd be surprised what I'd stoop to.' " I investigated for lawyers, but all of my work so far had been on civil cases.

"Well, I got one for you, if you're interested. Really need your help on this one."

I looked back toward the outer door, to the words LEGAL INVESTIGATIONS, INC. appearing backwards in big block letters on the frosted glass, to the pile of bills that I'd swept aside from under the mail slot when I opened it.

"My place or yours?" I'd have gone to Calcutta to meet him, but most lawyers made regular trips to the courts at the Daley Center, only two blocks from my building. Then, maybe sounding a little too anxious, I said, "You in your office?"

"Yeah."

"Actually I was just heading out to an accident scene on the north side, not far from you. I'll come by right now."

My office is only a few doors away from the La Salle Hotel Parking Garage, where I pay by the month. They give me my own reserved spot, which is actually better for them, since they valet park and I'm in and out all day long. I retrieved my car, a sexy red '84 Dodge Omni, seasoned with a hundred twenty-eight thousand miles and a little rust. I headed toward the Kennedy Expressway and slid down the northbound ramp.

Stanley Janda and I went to night law school together, both of us coppers at the time. I was working Homicide then; he had a cushy job in the superintendent's office downtown. After the bar exam he stayed on, eventually rose to become a deputy superintendent. Me, I got myself shot by a jealous husband and fired from the police department. I took two bullets that night, one through the ankle and one, I swear, through the lover's handle. The timing wasn't all that bad, since I'd just passed the bar exam. So, with a slight limp, I started practicing law a little earlier than Stan. The limp eventually disappeared, except on those occasions when I'd overtax my ankle, and I did well: made partner with a good firm, even developed a reputation as a hotshot trial lawyer.

Then I got disbarred.

I guess you could say I had some temper issues. The final straw came in the middle of a trial before Judge Walsh, a dim-witted ward heeler who frequently asked attorneys before him to explain the meaning of rather simple legal terminology. What I didn't know was that my opponent had contributed heavily toward Walsh's re-election campaign.

I might have looked the other way if they'd been a little subtle about it—some of that just goes with the territory. But seeing what he could get away with, my opponent pushed it, tried to ridicule me in front of the jury. When he publicly called me a liar, he'd crossed the line. I was on my feet objecting, and moved the court to admonish him.

Walsh laughed. "Sit down, Counsel. Why don't you just quit lying?"

My opponent snickered, and that tore it. With some fancy footwork I thought I could no longer muster on account of my bad ankle, I punched out the other lawyer right there; then the deputy sheriff charged to the rescue and I decked him, too; and I headed off the judge, who ran screaming from the bench, and laid him out right there. The jury never moved from their chairs.

The episode, of course, instantly ended my legal career.

After that, people began to regard me as unstable—I couldn't find a job doing anything. Stan Janda was practicing law too by then, one of the few people who stood by me. After Stan's high profile police career, he could pretty well have had his pick of the big firms, but to the surprise of everyone, he just hung out his shingle over an unassuming little storefront in the old Polish neighborhood on Milwaukee Avenue.

Stan had grown up in that neighborhood, though, had spoken Polish before he spoke English. He has a typical neighborhood practice: real estate, wills and trusts, divorce, a little personal injury—though he has a substantial criminal defense practice, too. Ironically, the scrambled eggs and gold braid he'd worn on his deputy superintendent's uniform cast a prospective light that didn't hurt his career as a criminal lawyer.

I found a parking spot on Milwaukee Avenue and walked half a block to Stan's office. It had none of the trappings you associate with a successful lawyer. Plain, generic, a copy machine and fax and secretary all in full view from the street, it could have been a real estate office or an insurance brokerage, or even, with a couple of posters, a travel agency.

"I'll tell him you're here," the receptionist said, and before I could sit down Stan's round-shouldered frame nearly filled the hallway, his oversized jaw slung into that half smirk, as though he was about to let you in on a joke.

"Come on back," he said, laying an arm on my shoulder. In his office, I took a chair in front of his desk and asked about his kids. Since I don't have kids, he asked how my business was doing.

"Terrific," I lied.

"Mike, believe me, I know how it is when you only get to eat what you kill—it's a rude awakening. But I went through it and I know you're going to do fine." His eyes shifted to the top of his desk and his mouth came open slightly.

"How are you feeling?" he asked. The question was not a formality. "How long has it been since, ah . . ." His voice trailed off.

"Since I got shot? It's okay, you can say it." He was not referring to the jealous husband incident, but something more recent. I seem to attract lead the way a magnet attracts iron filings. "It's nearly a year. It really wasn't too bad. If you remember, the bullet struck a tape recorder in my pocket."

14

"Can I say then that you really ought to be more careful?" He gave me that lopsided grin, but I could see he meant it. "Whatever happened with that, anyway? That guy who shot you, did he get sent away?"

I nodded, surprised he didn't know. I thought criminal lawyers had their own gossip network. "Yeah, but not because he shot me. I mean, that weighed against him in his plea bargain, but he went down for the murder in my client's apartment building. Anyway, the guy's in Pontiac now."

"For the murder, right. But he almost murdered you, too, didn't he? The guy that did it, he was a friend of yours, wasn't he?"

"Used to be."

"Mike, you got to find a better class of friends." He was smiling, leaning back, lacing his fingers behind his head. "I really need your help on this case, buddy. My client's charged with murder. If the State can prove its case—they've got a way to go, but if they can—he'll get the death penalty for sure. Would you like some coffee?"

"Sure, black," I said.

He called his secretary on the intercom, ordered two black coffees. "Client's name is Justin Ambertoe," he continued. "He's suspected of murdering a kid on the south side, Reggie Brockton, five years old. Thing is, they never found the body. They did find what looks like a murder scene in an abandoned apartment building on South Stewart, just around the corner from where the kid lived. Lots of blood in the basement. Last time Reggie's mother saw him he was headed around the block on his scooter. They found the scooter in the building, in an apartment on the first floor."

I got to my feet, walked to the window and looked out on the alley, at garage doors across the way. The banter about whether I'd work for a criminal defendant had been

15

just that, kidding around. But I wasn't sure I could work for a child killer. Even if I did need the work. Stan hadn't followed me with his eyes, but he must have known what I was thinking.

His secretary knocked on the door, then without waiting for an answer she came in, set two mugs of coffee on Stan's desk and left, closing the door behind her.

"You think he did it?" I asked without looking at him.

He turned to me now. "I'm a criminal lawyer. I don't really ask that."

I tried to think of a way to put it, then I just said, "But I'm asking you, Stan."

He rested an arm on the top of his desk. "If you don't think you can do it, it's all right. Really, Mike."

I went back and sat down and picked up my coffee mug, not sure what I wanted to say. Stan came forward in his chair like he was going to say something, but didn't; then his eyes shifted away and he released a rush of air. "No," he said, "I don't think he did it. In fact, I'd bet on it."

He sat back. "Let me tell you something. There's a whole lot of reasons why a criminal lawyer doesn't want to think about whether his client did the crime. People think it's because you don't want it on your conscience, getting a guilty guy off. No one stops to think that maybe you don't want it on your conscience when you can't save an innocent man from the death penalty. Look, I had a feeling you might have some reservations. I don't want you to even think about taking the case unless you can be one hundred percent committed."

I didn't think he meant any offense, but I said, "You really don't need to tell me that, Stan." I sipped my coffee. "Tell me about Ambertoe. What kind of guy is he?"

"He's a freelance photographer. Gets some pretty juicy assignments—*Architectural Digest, House Beautiful,* stuff like that. He's pretty mild-mannered, probably a little anal-retentive. Kind of shy."

"How did they link him to the murder?"

"A witness says he saw Ambertoe coming out of the building about the time the kid disappeared. Somebody got his license plate number. At first he denied being anywhere near the building." Stan cleared his throat. "Problem is, the cops got a search warrant for his apartment, and found photographs of the interior of the building."

"Oh, shit. Where does he live, by the way?"

"On Roscoe, near Clark Street."

I mentally mapped the coordinates. "Boys' town. He's gay?"

"Yeah."

"White?"

"Uh-huh."

I looked at Stan. He looked at me. "So what's a homosexual from boys' town doing in an abandoned building in Englewood?"

"He likes to photograph abandoned buildings. He was taking pictures that day. His big problem is, he lied to the police about being in the neighborhood."

"That puts him in pretty deep," I said, thinking maybe this was not a case for me.

"Yeah, it does. But the murder scene, I mean, the place where they found the blood, was in the basement. Justin claims he never went down to the basement."

"Is he locked up?"

"He hasn't been charged, not yet. The cops held him for a while, printed him and cut him loose. I'm not surprised. The State's Attorney's office needs a better case." He waited a beat, twirling a ballpoint pen in his fingers like a baton. "Mike, I need to know: Do you want to do this?"

"I assume he doesn't have a prior record?"

"Well, actually, he does. He served six years in prison."

Sometimes I'm not a very good poker player. I couldn't keep my eyes from widening a little. "What for?"

Stan dropped the pen onto his desk and sat back. "Well, it was, ah . . . child molestation."

"Oh, Christ." I got up and paced to the window again. A garage door rose, a good-looking blonde backed out a white Acura.

"Mike, sit, will you?"

I sat.

"It was a technicality; he was in high school, just turned seventeen. The victim, quote-unquote, was sixteen. I mean, they were classmates. You know, lovers. It was completely consensual. It just so happened that Justin's birthday came before the other kid's."

"Something doesn't add up here, Stan. He didn't do six years for that."

Stan had just taken a mouthful of coffee, and he pumped his head up and down, brushing a drop from his lower lip. He swallowed. "Oh, yes he did. I neglected to tell you, Justin's from rural Texas. Bible-thumping country, where you get baptized in the river and homosexuals are an abomination in the sight of The Lord." He studied me for a few seconds. I was still thinking. "Mike, I need to know. Are you in or not?"

I didn't like it, not one bit. But at a time when a lot of people I knew treated me like a puddle of puke on a picnic table, Stan and another lawyer stood by me. They couldn't save my law license—no one could have done that—but they kept my sorry Irish ass out of jail and, more importantly, made a miracle of a deal with the State's Attorney, a plea bargain which resulted in a fine and court supervision. No felony conviction, which would have kept me from ever holding a P.I. license.

"I'm in," I said. "I want to meet Ambertoe as soon as possible."

His face softened into a relaxed smile. "I'll call him this morning, tell him to contact you as soon as possible. Tell you what, my office is your office." He pushed back from his desk, pulled open the top drawer, rummaged around. "Here's a key," he said, dropping it on the desk in front of me.

"I've got an office."

"I know. But the file will be here, if you need it when I'm not here. In fact, there's a desk under all that crap piled in the other room, if you come in and need a place to work. I'll get it cleaned off."

"That's not necessary," I said, but I picked up the key, put it in my pocket.

"I've been going to clean up in there anyway," he said, and stood. "Thinking of hiring an associate." As he guided me to the front door, he asked, "Going deer hunting this fall?"

"I guess so. I've hardly missed a season since I was eighteen."

"That venison sausage you brought over last year, it was the hit of the Christmas party."

"I'll bring you another one this year. Assuming I kill a deer—remember what you said about only eating what you kill."

He laughed, and as we stood at the front door he started to say something, but caught himself. When I looked at him, his cheeks were flushed.

"What?" I said.

He eyed me for a couple of seconds. "I was going to say that if you ever get your law license back . . ." He gestured with his head back toward the unoccupied office. "I really mean it."

"Thanks, Stan. That won't happen any time soon."

CHAPTER TWO

I drove back to my office wondering about this guy Ambertoe, misgivings tugging at my gut, but acknowledging in my head that he had a right to a good lawyer as well as a decent investigator. The prosecution had a whole army of investigators trying to chill his ass forever.

I hadn't given a thought to deer hunting until Stan brought it up. I used to take two a year, one with a bow, another during rifle season, though in the past few years I'd only hunted with a bow. But bow-hunting season had already started, and I hadn't even bought my license. It was true I'd rarely missed the deer hunt, but something was changing in me.

Deer hunting was never a sport to me. It is something sacred, a death and life ritual which connects me to the earth, to the cosmos, to what it is to be alive and to provide sustenance. We buy our meat neatly packaged at the meat counter, consume it amazingly insulated from any idea of the animal as a living thing, from any thought of its death.

I know of no hunter who takes joy in killing; killing is not the object. Life is the object—the same life provided by the foodstuffs antiseptically wrapped at the Jewel.

And yet—though I still cling to that fundamental view, the pathos of the animal's death has grown in my heart each year, until it has become a matter of forcing myself to perform the rite. So long as I eat meat or wear leather, though, I cannot turn my face from the deed, cannot fail to acknowledge the life an animal gives so that we may sustain ourselves—

pretend, like a good German, that I have no connection with that death. We are all killers. Not even the hyena lives on carrion alone.

The hyena. Those black eyes glowing in the night were still in my head. Every day I scoured the papers, monitored the radio news station for any mention of the animal. Where could it have come from? If it had escaped from a zoo it would have been a big news story. An escaped pet? I never heard of a pet hyena—they are not exactly warm and cuddly. Besides, keeping one in the city was surely illegal. A circus? Never saw a hyena in a circus. And again, they wouldn't likely keep the escape a secret—unless it had been kept illegally. That had to be the answer. Whoever had been keeping that thing was afraid to report its escape.

It was now a week since I'd seen the animal, and my re-solve to tell no one about it was developing some cracks. How did it survive, caught as it was between two worlds?

I had thought of confiding in Beth, my ex-wife, but I hadn't talked to her in weeks. I couldn't just call her out of the blue and say, "Guess what I saw?" She thought I was quirky enough. There was one other person I might tell: my old partner, Marty Richter, now a watch commander at the Deering Police District. Marty and I still met for dinner regularly, and we do a weekend fishing trip a couple times a year.

When I got to my office the red message light was flashing on the answering machine. Justin Ambertoe, his voice formal, a little nervous, left his number. "I'd greatly appre-ciate your returning my call at your earliest convenience."

There being no other messages, my earliest convenience happened to be now. I dialed his number, then heard the distant approach of an elevated train, and hung up. The tracks are situated so that the wheels of the train pass just outside my window, not far above my head, the same elevated tracks which circumscribe the downtown area and provide its historic name: The Loop. My office is located on the wrong side of those tracks. Being outside the loop is a recurrent theme in my life.

The train screeched past, a variety of objects on my desk dancing to the music of its wheels, and as I waited to dial the phone again I caught Beth's eye, smiling over at me from the photo on the credenza. She seemed pleased that I was supporting myself, that I actually had clients. Well, one at the moment.

Ambertoe picked up the phone before it finished its first ring.

"This is Mike Duncavan," I said.

I hardly got my entire name out when he interrupted. "When can I see you, Mr. Duncavan?"

"Can you come by the office now? I'm on the southwest corner of Washington and Wells, second floor."

"I can be there in half an hour."

"Bring the photographs you took at the building. And some samples of your work, if you don't mind."

"I can't bring the prints; the police kept them. But I've got all the contact sheets in an album in my car."

I hung up, having second thoughts. I don't see many clients in my office, which wasn't exactly presentable. I've got more space than I need, a reception area without a receptionist, a vacant office next to mine. There's plenty of furniture, all of it left behind by the former tenant. The stuff's really not that bad. I'm pretty sure they bought it after World War II.

But everything was dusty. I don't have a cleaning service; I empty the wastebaskets myself, but I just never seem to get around to dusting. Now I considered going down the hall to the men's room, getting a couple of damp paper towels. I started toward the door when inspiration intervened. Or more like a distraction. I grabbed the phone, got two numbers from directory assistance, dialed the first one.

The lady who answered the phone at the Lincoln Park Zoo said they did not have hyenas. "I think we're going to get some, though," the helpful lady said, "when the Africa House Exhibit is finished. But that won't be for another two years."

I thanked her, dialed the Brookfield Zoo, again asked if they had hyenas. I was put on hold.

"Library," the lady answered.

"Sorry," I said, "I called to find out if the zoo kept hyenas. They connected me to you."

"That's right, I field those kinds of questions. Yes, we do have hyenas. The spotted," she said. "Is there a hyena moon out there or something? You're the second person today to call about hyenas."

"You mean somebody saw one loose?"

"No, no, no. The man just wanted to know if we were interested in buying one. When the director's not in, they send me those calls, too."

"Would you be, um, missing a hyena, by any chance?" I asked.

Silence, followed by a chuckle. "Missing a hyena? Not that I know of," she said with mock indignation. "Why, have you found one?"

"No," I said. "It's my wife, sometimes she forgets to take her medication." I hung up quickly, then felt the heat of Beth's eyes on me. *You're an ex-wife,* I told her. But then I couldn't take my eyes away from hers for a long time.

Beth and I had married young, when I was on the Chicago

Police Department and going to law school at night. She stuck by me through some bad times, through an infidelity that ended in a cataclysm of gunfire and death and disgrace. My failures have never been small ones. As I struggled to rebuild my life, she was there.

As a lawyer I got a big break, a job at a firm whose name went with prestige like Smith went with Wesson. I made partner fast, started enjoying the good life, expensive things. And I began to notice that glamorous women seemed to like me—Mike Duncavan, an Irish kid who grew up in back of the stockyards. Beth was pretty and clever and fun. She was good-humored and witty. But glamorous she was not—she said it herself. Once I wanted to buy her a full-length mink, and she just laughed. "I'm not the fur coat type," she said.

At the time, I still loved Beth, but a man of my position—it started affecting our sex life. In bed I would fantasize that Beth was a stranger, tall and blonde and stunning to look at. When we finally split, I gave her everything: the house, the Lexus, the bank accounts. I just kept her old Dodge Omni until I could get a new car.

At the dealership I found a cherry-red Corvette that was perfect for an up-and-comer like myself, and in the service department behind the cashier's window, I discovered a goddess, a part-time model who said she loved my taste in automobiles. She looked uncannily like the woman in my bedroom fantasies—long-legged, blonde, perfect body, an absolute knockout. We hit it off right away, were married in six months, divorced in a year. But even before the end, I found myself fantasizing in the sack once again—this time pretending that she was Beth. Now Madonna's driving my Corvette. I'm still driving the Omni.

Beth was crushed by the divorce, inconsolable. From her perspective it had really came out of nowhere, for no

24

reason. When it was over, she took a class in sculpture and ceramics, probably to take her mind off it, probably to meet someone new.

And she did meet someone new: an undiscovered side of herself, a person with abundant talent and imagination and the skills to market them. It seemed as if, like a trumpeter swan, she just molted, cast off the shy side of herself. She started selling a few pieces, and before long her work was in demand.

She moved to Sutler's Grove, bought an old Victorian house and set up a studio in the small barn behind it. She began by turning out tableaus of Norman Rockwell moments— a little girl holding a butterfly on the tip of her finger, a little boy with a fishing pole over his shoulder, that kind of thing. She discovered then that she could diversify, please a variety of tastes, and started another line, limited edition wildlife pieces in bronze that sold through outdoors catalogs.

Her business took off like a rocket. She hired assistants, making sure at the same time that some aspect of each piece was turned out by her own hand. Each piece was signed by her. I didn't want to know how much money she was making, but I was pretty sure it was more than I ever did in my best year. I had truly set her free.

You could say the trajectory of my own career was a lot like a rocket, too, if you thought of the *Challenger*. My law career rose steeply, then exploded in that great calamitous courtroom scene. After that, it was either employment as a legal investigator, or no employment at all.

Before Justin Ambertoe arrived, I got some wet paper towels and cleaned off the chair that faced my desk, one of those heavy wooden ones with the seat scooped out in the shape of your butt, then ran the soggy paper over the desk in the outer office.

CHAPTER THREE

Ambertoe's knock was so tentative I wasn't sure I'd heard it, but I answered anyway. He stood framed in the doorway clutching a thick, three-ring binder to his chest, not looking at all as I'd pictured him—slightly built, trim mustache, hair going gray at the temples, wearing a tweed sport coat that looked tailor-made, blue oxford cloth shirt open at the throat, tan Dockers, and penny loafers neatly shined. I guess I expected a guy who climbed around abandoned buildings to look a little more rugged.

I tried a warm smile and invited him in, quickly ushering him past the reception area to my office, and sat him down. He didn't smile back. I didn't even settle in behind my desk when he said, "I'd like to get the monetary arrangements out of the way first. Do I owe you some sort of retainer?"

"Your lawyer hired me. My arrangement is with him."

Before I could say anything more, he said, "There's one other thing. I'm the sort of person who likes to be up front, so please pardon me if I seem overly forward, I don't mean to be. I understand you're an ex-policeman?"

I nodded.

"And you know I'm ah, gay?"

I wasn't sure where this was going, but I said, "Right."

"So . . . is this going to work?"

"Sorry, I don't follow."

"Then let me speak plainly," he said, leaning an elbow on the arm of the chair. "Cops are usually right-wingers. Homophobic. I need to know up front: are you a homophobe, Mr. Duncavan?"

I looked at this guy, gave it a five count. Didn't he want to know if I was a right-winger, too? I kept the tone conversational. "Let *me* speak plainly," I said. "Homophobia's a word coined by some simple-minded fuck to communicate with other simple-minded fucks. I don't speak the language. But assume I'm a homophobe, whatever that means. That way you won't have to wonder. Now, as I see it, you are dangerously close to being indicted for a capital crime, and this homophobe is the only person, other than your lawyer, of course—surely another homophobe—who might keep you from smelling your own hair burn while you sizzle in the electric chair. So do you want me on this case?" Actually the Sovereign State of Illinois no longer used the chair, but I thought the image might be helpful—a matter of poetic license.

He shifted, looked down, eyes unfocused, but he didn't seem to lose composure. "You take me wrong," he said, a little sheepishly. "I just want certain things to be up front. If I offended you, I'm sorry."

Now it was my turn to feel sheepish. I never did take well to being stereotyped, and I'd probably been too hard on him. He'd surely endured some pretty ugly stuff at the hands of cops, let alone in that Texas jail. But at least we'd set some boundaries.

"No problem," I said. "Can I get you some coffee, pop, anything?"

"No, thank you," he said.

"Anyway, I need to be clear about one more thing, too. It's a question your lawyer won't ask you, but I need to know: did you have anything to do with that kid's disappearance?"

He was looking over my shoulder. "No." He said it absently, without looking at me. Then he looked me straight in the eye. "No, absolutely not."

"You were at the building, though?"

He nodded.

"Why did you lie to the police?"

He removed his eyes from mine and shook his head slowly, as though searching for an answer somewhere inside. "I guess I just panicked. It was stupid, but I was scared to death."

"The missing kid, did you ever see him?"

"No. I mean, I don't think so. The cops showed me his picture, but I really didn't pay much attention to anybody. I try to avoid eye contact when I'm working in a neighborhood like that; I was really nervous about just being there. Inside the building there was a lot of broken furniture and stuff lying around, which contributed to the atmosphere I was trying to capture. I thought the child's scooter made a nice touch. Kind of evocative of the apartment's former life. I just assumed it had been abandoned there, like everything else."

"Do you know what time you arrived, and what time you left?"

"Not exactly, but I wanted the afternoon sun coming through the west windows. I know I got there about three-thirty. I think it was about five-thirty when I left."

"How many times did you go there?"

"Only once. Well twice, actually, but the first time I just drove around scouting the neighborhood for abandoned buildings. I found this one, saw that the front door was wide open. Then I went back later with my camera."

"The same day?"

"No, two days later."

"Do you remember seeing anyone hanging around, either time?"

"There were people on the street, but no, no one in par-
ticular. That first time, I wasn't there more than two minutes, just got out of my car and went up the walk and
looked in through the front door. The second time, there
were people on the street, but as I said, I went out of my
way to avoid eye contact. I just grabbed my camera and
equipment and went in the front door. It was open. So was
the inner door, and the door to the apartment."

"Do you remember anything unusual happening, anything at all?"

"Not really. I mean, I can tell you a lot about the interior
of the building, but that's all I paid attention to."

"Except the basement?"

"Right, except the basement, I didn't go down there."

"Why not?"

He shrugged. "As I say, I wanted the afternoon sun
coming through the windows. I didn't think there'd be
much sunlight in the basement."

"Okay, here's what I want you to do. When you get
home, set aside some time and think real hard; try to remember every detail you can. Close your eyes and try to vi-
sualize it all in slow motion; retrace every moment in your
head. Who did you see, what did they look like. Vehicles
parked on the street, or driving by, try to remember. Then
write it down, every trivial thing that comes to mind; I don't
care how insignificant it might seem to you. Any detail
could mean a lot to me. Then call me tomorrow and replay
it for me. Okay?"

He seemed to warm up a little. His shoulders relaxed,
and he allowed himself the faintest smile. "Sure."

"Now, can I have a look at your pictures?"

For the first time he unclutched the binder from his
chest, opened it, removed several contact sheets, and

handed them to me. He worked with a large format camera, so even without enlargement, the detail was excellent. I found a magnifying glass in the drawer, went over each one. He was good, no doubt about that. They were all black-and-white, the natural light from the window spilling over the dark, empty room, the range of exposure perfect, good detail even in deep shadow.

He was right about the photographs featuring the scooter. That child's toy, so innocent against the backdrop of decay, made for some moving images. Then I noticed something. The scooter was in different places in different photographs.

"You moved the scooter, right?"

"Yes. Why, do you think that's cheating?" He gave me a look that could only be described as coy. It annoyed me a little, but at least he was loosening up.

"That means you probably left fingerprints on it. Can I have a look at some of your other work?"

"Yes, but first let me . . ." He opened the binder, paged through it. "I don't think you'll like these," he said, and started to remove some pages.

"Never mind, I promise not to be judgmental." I reached for the binder.

"Are you sure?" He closed it, offered it tentatively. "There's quite a bit of erotica."

I shrugged. "I'm a big boy."

"Gay erotica?"

I withdrew my hand. "Why don't you take those out?" I said.

After seeing Justin to the door and saying goodbye, I went to my chair and turned it to the window, which faces diagonally across the intersection. The sidewalk on Washington Street just one floor below teems with pedestrians, and no one ever looks up. In the morning, before nine, you can look straight down on hordes of stunning secretaries in their low-cut apparel as they wait, oblivious, just below my window for the light to change. Oblivious to the lascivious. Okay, I'm a dirty old man. But I'm still a good person.

And as I sat there, Ambertoe swung into view below with that binder still pressed to his chest. He scurried across Washington as the light started to change, rotating his hips like a woman in a tight dress. And suddenly I was overwhelmed with the need to protect him. He was innocent, I was sure of it. I had no doubt that he went to the building as a photographer—he had the credentials, the mastery of light and contrast and subtlety. And I did not believe he could have been an opportunistic killer, driven by a passion of the moment. If that were the case, would he have hung around and photographed his victim's scooter? And done so with such sensitivity? There was not a chance in hell he was guilty, and that fact suddenly lay like a heavy weight on my shoulders.

CHAPTER FOUR

After leaving the office, I stopped for a couple of drinks at Monk's Pub on Lake Street, giving the Loop time to disgorge its bloated parking garages, then picked up my car and drove home. I live in Bucktown, in a second-floor apartment on McClean, a green clapboard bungalow that sits, like all the houses on the block, below sidewalk level. My landlord, Fred Habranek, is a retired fireman, a widower who lives on the first floor with his cat, Butler. Lucky for me, Fred is crazy about Stapler, and gives him the run of the back yard.

I opened a can of Dinty Moore stew and heated it on the stove, ate it with some French bread and a bottle of beer while I watched the History Channel. Then I took Stapler for a walk, and went to bed early.

That night I awoke from a deep slumber, sure I heard a sound in the house. I listened, the moon pitching a long triangle of light across my bed. There was only the sound of the refrigerator coming on, and I went back to sleep.

Then I awoke again, to the slow tick of claws crossing the oak floor toward my bedroom. It stopped. I squinted in the semi-darkness through the open door, pulse pounding in my temples. There was nothing there.

But then I noticed that the shard of moonlight had taken on a different shape and I saw it then, on the light's fringe, head held low, the glint of the hyena's black eye focused on mine. Now the animal inched closer, moving into the room, teeth bared, head weaving for a better look at me.

I started to sit up, and that's when I discovered I was paralyzed, could not even move an eyeball. In the periphery of my vision, the thing drifted toward the head of the bed, then out of sight. I waited, terrified, the sound of panting filling my ears from somewhere behind my head. Now its hot breath flickered on my ear, the stench of it surging into my nostrils.

And now its wet mouth was on my face.

That released me. I bolted upright, seized its throat, heaved it to the floor.

And Stapler let out a yelp of betrayal so keen that it splintered my heart. Poor fella only wanted to go out.

I let him out in the back yard, waited in the kitchen until he scratched on the door to come back in, and gave him a handful of Milk Bones, a meager apology. Then I went back to bed and, for the rest of the night, slept with the light on.

CHAPTER FIVE

In the morning before the sun was up, I rode my bike over to Humboldt Park, pedaling fast through the maze of drives, and when I came back I did the rowing machine for ten minutes, then another ten on the speed bag. When I was younger I was a jogging nut, ran the Chicago Marathon three times. But the bullet through my ankle ended that forever. Now I alternate: a cardiovascular workout one day, weights and the heavy bag the next. One of the two bedrooms in my small apartment is dedicated to workout equipment, and Fred lets me hang the heavy bag in the basement.

I showered and sat at the kitchen table with the *Sun-Times* and the first cup of coffee of the day, Stapler crunching Purina Dog Chow at my feet.

A story in the paper made me resolve, by one of those meandering paths of association, to call Marty Richter first thing when I reached the office. It had been awhile since we'd met for dinner. The article was about a mid-sized scandal at Glen Oaks, a west side nursing home. A number of unmarked graves had been discovered on the grounds there, behind the big, old mansion. No suggestion of foul play—the bodies seemed to be those of former residents who'd passed on at the nursing home with no known next of kin. The state in such cases paid a modest sum to the nursing home to make the burial arrangements. It seemed that for years Glen Oaks had been conducting its own abbreviated, back yard interments and pocketing the money. There were quite a number of cadavers, some old, some recently deceased. Many of the graves were fairly shallow, with bodies stacked one on top of the other.

I thought Marty Richter probably had the inside scoop, because he happened to be temporarily detailed to the police district where Glen Oaks is located. But the connection went deeper. When Marty and I worked homicide back in the eighties, we were called to Glen Oaks once.

Facing Humboldt Park, its wrought iron fence falling down here and there, the place even then had an air of elegance gone to seed. But once inside, you'd think you'd stepped into purgatory: large, open wards housing row upon row of discarded human beings, every hallway echoing with the moans of abandoned souls. Marty and I were there to look into the death of an elderly woman whose family claimed she'd died of neglect. But she'd reached her late nineties when she passed on. There was simply no proof of neglect.

But neither Marty nor I ever quite got the stench of that place out of our nostrils. Walking back to the squad car that day, we agreed that it would be really great to drop dead of a massive heart attack about age fifty.

I called Marty when I reached the office. "Did you catch the article about Glen Oaks this morning?" I asked.

"Yeah, made me think of calling you. Still want to kick off by age fifty?"

"I've decided to push the, ah, deadline a little. How about dinner tonight?"

We agreed to meet at The Old Barn, a restaurant on the southwest side, at seven.

I had no sooner hung up when Justin Ambertoe called. "I did what you told me," he said, "tried to think of everything I saw when I was at the building. I'm afraid there isn't much to report. Except I did remember one thing."

I waited for him to go on, but when he didn't, I said, "What's that?"

"Actually I did speak to someone, just momentarily. As I came up the walk that first time, this guy was standing near the front entrance of the building. I mean, I didn't know if he had anything to do with the building or not. So I asked him if he knew who the owner was. He said no, he didn't."

"That's it?"

"Yeah, then I went into the building."

"That was the first time you were there? You weren't carrying your camera equipment with you that time, right?"

"Right."

"What did the guy look like?"

"He was very good-looking. African, I think; he had a heavy accent. I don't know from which country. He was very dark-skinned, I'd say five-ten, a hundred seventy pounds. The muscles in his arms were well-defined. He had a pleasant smile, real white teeth. Seemed like a friendly fellow."

"What was he wearing?"

"Oh, good point. He had on a blue dashiki, cotton, with some kind of yellow pattern. His hair was cut real short."

"How old?"

"No more than forty. Not a single gray hair that I could see."

"Anything else you can remember about him?"

"Well, his name was David. David something," he said.

David something? What was this? Something was not computing.

"Hello?" he said.

"How do you know his name?"

There was a brief silence. "I introduced myself, when I

36

asked if he knew who owned the building, and he told me his name. I remember it was David something. I think his last name started with a *K*."

"You introduced yourself?"

"Yeah, I thought he had something to do with the building. That's about it."

Ambertoe was beginning to seem an odd duck. And strange as it appeared, all this seemed completely within his character.

"What about vehicles on the street. Do you remember anything?"

"I thought about that. Yeah, I did remember one, a blue van, kind of beat-up."

"Was that the first or second time you were there?"

"Both times. It was parked in front of the building."

I thanked him and hung up, feeling a little uneasy about Ambertoe's possible lack of candor. Why didn't he remember "David" during my first interview? But at least he took careful notice of young men. That could turn out to be helpful.

A light rain was falling when I arrived at The Old Barn to meet Marty Richter, though not enough to require an umbrella as I hurried to the entrance. Converted from an enormous old barn, it is said to have started its second life as a speakeasy in the twenties. Its interior is labyrinthine, and I walked through the main door down a corridor lined with red leather chairs, the soft light of its honey walnut paneling suffused with the mellow optimism of the jazz age, to a heavy door at the end, which did indeed have a peephole at its center. But you didn't need a secret knock, or any knock. That door opened into a sort of club room, subdued lighting, more elegant walnut and red leather chairs, and a hostess standing behind a green-shaded lamp with her reservation book.

There are three dining rooms, but I went into the bar to

look for Marty. I spotted him on a stool at the far end studying a martini, his fingers laced across the span of his belly, his thick, silver hair glistening like flax under canister lighting that accentuated the sag of his jowls. He didn't see me. He poked out his jaw as I approached, allowing smoke to curl up from his lower lip. I slid onto the stool next to him, and his jowls quivered a little as he swung his face around. He raised his glass. "I started without you," he said.

I ordered a double Stoli on the rocks, and told him about the Ambertoe case.

"You've crossed over to the dark side," he said. When I didn't respond, he put his drink down. "Think he did it?"

"No."

He looked me in the eye. "Well, I do."

I shifted my eyes off his, changing the subject only slightly, and told him how Ambertoe asked if I was a homophobe.

Marty smiled at that. "Who was it said, 'The corruption of man follows the corruption of language'?"

"Ralph Waldo Emerson, I think. Another happy fella."

He shook his head. "Might've been Emerson, but you're confusing him with Whitman. Whitman was the one who wrote love poems to his pal."

We ordered another round of drinks, and I brought up the subject of Glen Oaks. "You think they'll finally shut the place down?" I asked.

He stubbed out a cigarette. "Beats me," he said. "But the papers never mentioned the most interesting part of the story—how the bodies came to be discovered in the first place." Marty sat back with a hint of a smile, waiting for me to ask him about it.

"Okay, so how were they discovered?"

"Well, I was talking to Harry Potts, the watch commander on afternoons. Someone passing by the place yesterday morning spotted what looked like some bones lying on the lawn inside the fence, and called the police. The beat car that responded found them, then found a lot more. I guess they were lying all over the place. Then the guys found the graves that had been dug up, in back of the house.

"But here's the thing: Potts said the corpses had been dug up by some kind of an animal. Some powerful animal. Said it looked like whatever did it could've competed with a backhoe."

The skin at my temples began to crawl. Marty sipped his martini, sat back and squinted at me. "What's the matter with you?"

"Nothing, why?"

"You look like you just remembered you left something cooking on the stove."

"No, it's nothing. What kind of an animal, do you think?"

He shrugged. "Who knows? I'm just surprised the papers didn't pick up on *that*. Probably the reporters never asked the right questions."

I shifted, debating whether to tell him about the hyena in the park. It was time. "Marty, remember when we were kids, how I could name all the African animals in alphabetical order?"

"Yeah. My eyes would glaze over before you got to Bongo."

"A large, striped, forest-dwelling antelope."

Marty's head lolled back; he made a snoring sound.

I laughed. "Listen, I got to tell you something." I hesitated, hoping to convey a sense of gravity. "Something you're probably not going to believe."

He flipped open his Zippo with the Marine Corps emblem, lit a cigarette, angled his face away and blew out a stream of smoke. "What?"

"I was walking Stapler one night last week in Humboldt Park, and I saw something."

"You walk your dog at night in Humboldt Park? What're you, nuts?"

I waved a hand. "You want to hear this?"

"Okay. You saw something in the park. What was it?"

"A hyena," I said.

"A hyena." He fought back a grin. The grin won.

"Marty, look, I know it sounds crazy, but I know what I saw. It was close; I had my flashlight. I had a perfect view. Listen, I haven't told this to anybody. But Glen Oaks happens to be right across the street from the park. And hyenas are known to dig up graves."

I could tell Marty was impressed by the way his eye wandered in search of the bartender. He caught his attention, drew a circle with an index finger over our drinks. The bartender nodded.

"So what do you think?" I said.

He cocked his head. "Honestly?"

"Yeah, honestly."

"I think you saw a big, stray dog in the park that looked like a hyena."

"Marty, it was a hyena."

"No, it wasn't."

"I know it was."

"Okay, you saw a hyena." He took a deep drag on his cigarette, put it down, exhaled. "Look, I'm gonna test your memory, see if you remember this." Marty had a way of talking in a circle to emphasize a point. Sometimes the circle was way too big for the point.

" 'The Man Who Saw Everything Twice,' " he said drawing out the words of the clue. Marty also loved trivia questions. "Where's that from?"

"Easy," I said. "*Catch-22*, wasn't it?"

"Very good."

"I don't remember anything about that part, just the name."

"Well, the doctors converged on this patient, all trying to diagnose his problem, which was that he was seeing everything twice. The first doctor confirmed that it was meningitis. Now," he poked the air with a finger, "do you remember how he came up with that diagnosis?"

"Wasn't it because he was a meningitis man?"

"Excellent!" He sat back with a self-satisfied grin. "Another doctor asked him how he knew it wasn't, say, acute nephritis. And he said, 'Because I'm a meningitis man, not an acute nephritis man, and I got here first.' "

"How do you remember this shit?"

On a roll, he ignored me. "And *you're* an African animals man. That's why you saw a hyena. It's all up here, for Christ sake." He tapped his temple, then sat back, his smile a little too self-satisfied.

"And what do you think dug up those graves?"

"Not a hyena." He shook his head, blew a puff of air from his nose.

I picked up my glass, drained the last of the Stoli. "I know it was a hyena. There's no doubt about it. I guess what I'm asking you is: do you think I should report it?"

"Report it? Like, to the police?"

"Yeah."

"In a word, no," he said, picking up his lighter and cigarettes from the bar.

The bartender brought us two more drinks, which we carried into the dining room. We ate dinner and talked of many subjects, but no more of the hyena in the park.

CHAPTER SIX

The next morning I drove south on the Dan Ryan, got off at Garfield Boulevard, and cut over to Englewood, wanting to get a look at the abandoned building where Justin had taken the photos, the one where the kid was supposed to have been murdered. It occurred to me, since Stan and I weren't at all sure exactly how much the police had on Justin, that we'd almost be better off if the police had charged him. At least then we'd have access to all the information the police had. Did they know anything we didn't? It was a cinch they didn't think they had enough to make murder one stick, not yet.

I turned onto south Stewart and found myself disoriented. It had to be the right block, but something wasn't right—there was a vacant lot at the corner where the building was supposed to be. I cruised down the street, slowly realizing that I was in the right place—the building was simply gone, torn down. All that remained was a field of broken bricks and a lot of open air.

I parked in front of the newly vacant lot and got out, the street lined with frame bungalows and two-flats; a few empty spaces between them like gaps in a poor man's teeth. Where there should have been lawns, there was only dirt sparkling with broken glass. Six-flat buildings stood on the three other corners.

On the opposite side of the street, next to the corner apartment building, stood a bungalow with light blue aluminum siding. I crossed to it, mounted the front stairs and raised a finger to ring the bell, then saw the unconnected wires sticking out under the button. I rapped on the screen door, which set off a frenzy of barking.

"Shut the fuck up!" a man shouted. "Get back in there." The sound of dog nails scraping linoleum, then a few seconds later one side of the shade moved sideways, exposing one half of an angry black face. "Whatchew want?"

"I need to talk to you about the missing boy."

"Well, I told y'all everything I know," he said, but there was the sound of locks coming undone. If he thought I was the police, there wasn't any point in setting him straight. He swung the door open and stood glaring from behind the screen in a white undershirt, arms crossed, a wiry, dark-skinned man, his pinched cheeks graveled with shaving bumps. "Ain't you the same guy was here before?"

I shook my head. "No, there's lots of us working on this. Sorry to bother you again, but we really need to get as much information as we can, to find the missing boy."

He snorted. "Missing boy," he said. "That boy dead, you know it, and I know it. That white muthafucka killed him, sure as you're standing there. You had the guy, and y'all just turn him aloose."

"We couldn't charge him, there wasn't enough evidence. We need the community's help, need to get enough evidence to convict him. Otherwise, he'll beat it in court and be back on the street."

"Well, he back on the streets now, ain't he?"

"Can I have your name again, Mister . . . ?" I held pen to notebook.

"Bonnerly. I gave you my name once't. Now watchew want from me?"

"Look, we want whoever did this locked up just as much as you do. Please just tell me again what you remember about the white man, or anyone else you might have seen around the building. Anybody who might have looked suspicious."

He seemed to cool down a little, went from a rolling boil to a slow simmer. "Like I told y'all, I seen the guy hangin' round over there. The fuck a white man be doin' hanging round here anyhow? He don't belong round here. Let me just go up around your neighborhood, stand around on the corner, you know what? Po-lice have my black ass in jail quicker'n shit. Soon's I heard that child was missing, I knew he took that boy. That's when I called, gave y'all the license number. And y'all just up and let him go. Why? I'll tell you why, 'cause he *white,* that's why. Bin a black man, his ass'd be rottin' in jail right now." He was getting steamed again.

"Why don't we work together on this?" I said. "We both want the same thing."

"You know yourself, it had to be a white man done it, took that poor little child. You ever hear of a black man do like that? Ever hear of a black John Wayne Gacy? Or a Jeffrey Dahmer? Or a, whatsizname, dude cut up all them nurses?"

"No, but if we're going to convict him, we need your help. How many times did you actually see the man?"

"Did you talk to that African guy across the street?"

"African guy?"

"Yeah, he was talking to the white dude like they was friends or something. Guy stay with Mrs. Overhill, at the rooming house over there across the street." He pointed to a two-story stucco, mid-block.

"You saw them talking? For how long?"

"Man, you think I got nothing better to do than stand around all day with a stopwatch and my nose in other people's bidness?"

44

I wanted to say yes, but didn't. "How many times did you see the white guy?"

"I seen him over there three, maybe four times."

"You're sure? Three or four?"

"I'm sure it was three times, maybe more. He got no bidness hangin' round here. He got to be up to no good, why else he here?"

I jotted a note to myself. "And how many times did you see him talking to the African guy?"

"I just seen them out there talking the one day. Stood there musta been a half-hour, at least. The damn fool shoulda known the white dude was up to no good."

"When you say African, do you mean . . ."

"I mean the guy be from Africa, the fuck you think I mean? He talks funny."

"Do you know his name?"

"No, I don't know his name, I never spoke to the man, just heard him talk to people in that funny accent. But he live right there, why'nt you go over there and talk to him yourself? Now I got to go." He shut the door.

I headed across the street, past a rusty Buick squatting on blocks with its windows broken out, to the stucco house. One end of a rain gutter hung down, broken loose from the porch roof. At the front door the sound of a vacuum cleaner stopped when I rang the bell.

You might not think a two-hundred-fifty-pound woman could be pretty, but she was—taller than me, about thirty-five, skin like Dutch chocolate, breasts like a couple of soccer balls. She had eyes that made you want to rest your head in her cleavage and tell her all your troubles.

"You're here about that missing boy?" she said through the screen door, her face soft with compassion.

45

"I'm sure you've been interviewed already, but I just have a few more questions."

"Why don't you come in?" She swung the screen door open and I followed her into a small living room that smelled of furniture polish, an upright vacuum cleaner standing in the middle of the carpet. "I'm so sorry for that child's mother. Lord, what she must be going through, I can't imagine," she said. "Whatever I can do to help."

"Can you think of anything you may have noticed happening around that building, anything at all? I know the police already asked you, but sometimes people remember things after they've thought it over."

"I've thought about it a lot. I wish I could tell you something that would help, but I just never paid no attention." Her face brightened. "Did you speak to Mr. Bonnerly, across the street? He pretty well knows everything goes on around here."

"Yeah, he said there's a man living here with you that spoke to the man the police arrested. An African man?"

"Mr. Akibu?" She nodded. "I don't know about him talking to the man, but he don't live here no more. He stayed here maybe two months. I rent rooms by the week or the month. Nobody stays very long."

"Akibu?" I wrote the name down. "Do you know where he moved to?"

She looked disappointed. "No, I sure don't. If people don't tell me, I don't ask."

"What do you know about him?"

"Not much. He was polite. And clean. Paid his rent, kept pretty much to himself, wasn't no kind of trouble."

"What did he do for a living?"

"Import business, way I understood it, African wood carvings, jewelry, things like that. Oh," she put a finger to

46

her chin, then pointed at an animal skin draped over a small table, "that was a gift from Mr. Akibu. I don't know what kind of animal it is, but it's beautiful, don't you think?"

"Springbok," I said, proud of myself. The skin was in nice condition, a deep russet edged with a strip of dark brown and a second strip of pure white, mounted on black felt. "What about birth date or Social Security number? Do you have any records?"

"No, I'm afraid I don't. Why? You don't think Mr. Akibu had anything to do with that little boy?"

"No, just trying to gather as much information as we can," I said.

"I don't have no leases, nothing like that. People pay me cash. Most people stay here don't even have a checking account. Sorry."

"It's okay. Did Mr. Akibu tell you anything more about his background—what country he's from, how long he's been here?"

"No, I'm afraid he didn't."

"Any family that you know of?"

She shook her head slowly, like a school kid who wasn't getting any right answers. "I sure wish I could tell you more, but I try to stay out of my tenants' business. Long as they behave and pay their rent. Mr. Akibu had a strong accent, sometimes I couldn't even understand him. Beyond that, I can't tell you."

"Do you know his first name?"

"David," she beamed. "I know that much. David Akibu."

"Was Mr. Akibu friendly with any other tenants?"

"Yes, I should have thought to tell you. Kimberly Price. They was . . . real friendly."

"Is Ms. Price home, by any chance?"

She gave me that look of disappointment again. "She moved out, too, couple of weeks ago—she left before Mr. Akibu. Kimberly's a cosmetologist, but she got laid off from her job. She found something else on the north side, and she's moved up there somewhere."

"Look, here's my card. If you hear from either one of them, will you call me?"

"I certainly will," she said, then looking at my card, she said, "Oh," as though she were startled. "You're not a policeman?"

"No ma'am, I'm a private investigator. But we're all working for the same thing."

By her smile she seemed to accept that. Glad I didn't have to explain who I was working for, I thanked her, and as we went to the door she asked, "Do you think there's any chance the boy could still be alive? That poor mother. I just can't stop thinking about what she must be going through."

"There's no way to know," I said. But I was pretty sure I knew.

When I got back to the office, I called Justin Ambertoe, related what Bonnerly told me about his long conversation with David Akibu. "Are you sure you didn't talk to him longer?" I asked.

"No." Then he paused. "I really don't see what difference it makes." He was really beginning to irritate me.

"No, you didn't, or no, you're not sure."

"No, I'm sure. Maybe I talked to him for a half-minute. It was probably less."

"Okay, from now on, let me worry about what difference it makes. I need to know every single detail. I never know what might turn out to be significant later on."

"I'm sorry."

48

"The man also said you were at the building three or four times. Think, Justin. Could it have been more than twice?"

I didn't like the fact that he seemed to be thinking this over.

"No, it was twice," he said finally.

I said goodbye, troubled by his hesitation.

CHAPTER SEVEN

I checked both directory assistance and the phone book for a David Akibu, no luck. I'd hit a brick wall, and hit it early.

Then a week later, about two in the afternoon, Marty Richter called me from the station. He was just finishing his shift on the day watch. He'd started early, overlapping the change of watches, to keep continuity between the men going off and coming on.

"Listen," he said, "I got to tell you about something that happened last night, on the midnight shift." For some reason he was keeping his voice low. "Remember what you told me about seeing the, ah . . . something in the park?"

There were loud voices in the background. "Just a minute," he said. He must have covered the mouthpiece with his hand. I heard his muffled voice, then a long pause. When he came back, he said, "There's too many people standing around, I'll call you from home. I think you'll want to hear this."

Marty called back an hour later.

"A beat car on midnights spotted a couple of white guys that looked like cowboys," he said, "cruising around Humboldt Park in a red pickup truck. Texas plates, a rifle rack hanging in the back window. No rifles, of course, but they were driving real slow. The beat car pulled them over. These guys had a couple of dog kennels in the back, and they had a dog noose behind the seat, and get this: a tranquilizer gun."

"So, what was their story?"

"We don't know. They handed over their driver's licenses, polite as hell. But when the patrol officer asked them what they were doing, all they would say was that they were sightseeing."

"How did they explain the tranquilizer gun?"

"They didn't. They just said, 'We'd rather not say.' "

I mulled it over. "They must have known they'd look like they were hiding something. You'd think they'd at least have made something up."

"Yeah, but the guys said they didn't seem like criminal types, just rural types. Like a couple of cowboys, as I said. The night field lieutenant told me about it, just kind of off-hand, and so I talked to the officers at check-off. They said the guys weren't acting nervous or anything. They probably just couldn't think up a story fast enough, so, better to politely say, 'None of your business,' than get caught in a lie. They weren't breaking any laws. The beat guys just took down their names and license number and let them go."

"Did you get the names?"

"Yeah. I suppose you want them?"

"Sure."

"What're you planning to do with this, Mike?"

"Doesn't it bother you that you could have a wild hyena running loose in your district?"

"I got every kind of scum-sucking dirt bag you can think of running loose in my district. It would be an improvement. You want the information?"

"Yeah."

"Truck's registered to Mesquite Bend Ranch, Incorporated. The guys' names are Nate Wilcox and Elmer Bumpp, both from Texas." He spelled the names. "They're staying at the Fiftieth on the Lake Motel."

We said goodbye, then when I started to hang up, he said, "Mike, wait a minute."

"Yeah?"

"Where you going with this, buddy?"

I wasn't ready to tell him, but he asked. "I know you think I'm crazy, but it can't hurt to talk to these guys."

"You're right. I think you're crazy. Haven't you got anything better to do?"

I hung up, a hunch like a shot of raw bourbon chewing at my gut. I suddenly remembered the Outdoor Sports and Travel Show—didn't the Mesquite Bend Ranch have a booth there?

Every spring, in a mania of wishful thinking, I attended the show and lugged home a bagful of brochures: fly-in muskie fishing in Ontario, wing shooting in Nebraska, back-country elk hunting in Montana. The bag usually sat in the back of the closet until the following year's show. I couldn't have named a single outfitter if Regis Philbin was asking the question, but one of them was so out of the ordinary it stuck in my memory, and I was pretty sure the outfit was called Mesquite Bend Ranch.

Curiosity had drawn me over to the booth that afternoon, to a sand-table model of an African outpost. The guy in the booth, wearing a big, pearl cowboy hat, string tie, and black leather vest, gave me a down-home smile and asked, "Have you ever thought about hunting African game?" His drawl seemed odd. Safari outfitters nearly always spoke with a British accent, or at least South African.

Actually in better days, I *had* thought about it, at least enough to learn that political stability made some countries better destinations for big game hunting than others. "Where're you located?" I asked.

"How does Texas sound?" He was beaming, all teeth.

"Airfare's a damn sight cheaper, you don't have all the hassle with customs and immigration, like you do going in and out of foreign countries. Yet and still, the terrain and the climate are just about the same as Southern Africa." He unfolded a brochure, placed a finger on a picture of a herd of antelope. "We got twenty thousand acres, thirteen species of hooved animals. They're all free-roaming, wild as can be. Hell, you get yourself back in some a them arroyos, you can't tell if you're in Texas or Timbuktu."

I was pretty sure Timbuktu was a city, probably without arroyos. "Any natives?" I asked. I had the feeling this might be one of those places that buys tame animals from zoos for rich "sportsmen" to bag.

He cocked his head, his eyes never betraying whether he thought I was a wise-ass or just stupid, and didn't miss a beat. "It's no people back there," he said. "Just you and the animals. And your guide, a course."

That was the last show I'd been to, nearly four years before. In my current financial condition, I hadn't expected to be traveling to any exotic destinations anytime soon, so gave the show a pass. Now, as soon as I got home after talking to Marty, I went straight to the closet and located the bag of dusty brochures, dumped them out on the kitchen table and sorted through.

And I found it, the brochure with the caption: "Mesquite Bend Ranch: The safari of your dreams!"

Before I read it, I took three Lean Cuisine dinners from the freezer, put them in the microwave, and when they were done I piled the contents on a plate, popped the top off a Guinness and ate at the kitchen table, reading over the brochure. It told about the variety of antelope, and it occurred to me that they might have really been wild animals.

But so what? I realized, with self-doubt circling the edges of my mind, that none of this had anything to do with Justin Ambertoe and the missing child. What I seemed to be doing was avoiding a hard look at my progress. Still, there was some connection between the hyena and those cowboys cruising Humboldt Park in a pickup truck with a dog noose.

For the second time, my resolve not to tell anyone about the hyena was weakening. I had told Marty, whom I could trust to tell no one else. But he just dismissed me as a nut case. Now I considered calling Beth; she was the world's greatest listener.

By the time I'd finished supper and put the plate and the silverware in the sink, I'd dismissed calling her as a bad idea; then, as I squirted dish soap over them and washed them under running water, I could see her smile, hear the soft, comforting lilt of her voice. And before I knew it, my longing for her was keen.

I put the dishes away, took the portable phone to the living room couch and dialed her number. One ring, two rings, three rings. *Please, please be there, Beth.*

She answered then, and I was astonished by the depth of my relief. "Mike who?" she said, chiding me, her laugh as bright as a waterfall.

"I've been really busy," I said. Lord, that was lame. "Have I got you at a bad time?"

"No-o?" she said, her inflection making it a question.

"So how's business?"

"Business is fine." She laughed. "Did you really call to ask about my business?"

"I did."

"You did." A statement, followed by a pause freighted with doubt.

"No," I said. "I want to talk to you about a case I'm working on. I'd like your opinion."

She didn't hesitate. "Sure," she said. "I'm all ears."

"I've got to warn you, this is going to sound really, really bizarre."

"I doubt it. I'm talking to Mike Duncavan."

"Okay, then. But you've got to reserve judgment until the end."

"All right," she said. "Tell me."

I wasn't sure where to begin. Finally I said, "One night a few weeks ago, I took Stapler for a walk in Humboldt Park, and I saw a hyena."

No reaction.

"You there?" I said.

"Yes, go on. I'm reserving judgment, remember?"

I told her the whole story, then, about Justin Ambertoe and the missing boy, and the guys in the pickup truck cruising the park. Then I told her I thought there was a connection between the hyena and the African and the missing kid.

When I finished, she didn't say anything.

"What do you think?" I finally asked.

She still didn't answer, not right away. Then: "Did you talk to Marty about this?"

"Yeah."

"What does he think?"

"He thinks I'm crazy. Especially since no one's seen the hyena but me."

Another five seconds passed. Then she said, "There's no doubt in my mind, you saw a hyena in the park."

"You're putting me on."

"No. Here's what I'm thinking about, Mike. Whenever we used to go out in the country, you and I? Whether we were alone or with other people, you were always the one who saw things no one else saw. You would point them out to everybody, a deer at the edge of the woods, maybe, or a wild turkey, or a rare bird. A gopher or a chipmunk—everyone thought that was remarkable. No one else would ever notice these things unless you pointed them out. I used to think about that—that you had a rare gift. Maybe it's the difference between looking and seeing, I don't know. Maybe it has something to do with keener eyesight. Mike, how many people get to be as old as you and don't need glasses?"

"Now there's a compliment," I said.

Her laugh was a tonic. "I used to wonder if you just had the habit of looking for things where other people paid no attention, or if you had a way of never taking for granted what you were looking at, or what it was. I think your brain just—works differently." She reflected a moment on that, and giggled.

"Thanks," I said.

"No, but look. Marty says no one else saw it? But maybe other people *did* see it and didn't know what they were looking at. It's probably got something to do with how we process information. Normal people . . ." Another pause, another laugh.

"You're full of compliments tonight," I said.

"No, listen. Normal people see something like that, they expect that it's a dog. So that's what they see, a dog. It's not a conscious thing. People unconsciously avoid—what's it called again?" She reflected. "Cognitive dissonance."

"Cognitive dissonance?"

"Yeah. I think that's what they call it. I'm reaching back to a college psych course." She stopped talking. I didn't say anything, not sure she'd finished. She hadn't.

"Another thing," she went on. "You said yourself, you did

56

not want to report it. So maybe other people saw it, and maybe they didn't report it, either. Did you ever think of that?"

"No," I said.

"Well, there you are," she said confidently, though where I was I wasn't exactly sure. Especially after her next question.

"The part I'm not getting, Mike, is—where does the hyena, and the cowboys in the pickup truck, where do they all fit in with your client and the missing little boy?"

"Well, this African that Justin spoke to, the one he met in front of the building, he's in the import business. He imports stuff from Africa." And in the silence I felt my face grow warm. Out loud, it sounded so lame.

"Oh, I see," she said in a tone that said she didn't see at all. She paused again, and in the silence I felt my face grow even warmer. But then she shifted into a more intimate register. "How're you doing, Mike? Really, you okay?"

The softness of her voice thrilled me, and I fought back an urge to voice sentiments welling up from deep inside: *I miss you. I need you. Let's try again.* "I'm doing great," I said. "My business is really starting to take off."

"Glad to hear it," she said. "I knew all along you'd do well."

Now I was listening to silence. It was my nickel, and I didn't want to say goodbye.

"Does that about cover it, Mike, what you called about?"

"Yeah, thanks, Beth," I said.

"Well, call me if you want to talk again."

"Good night," I said. I started to hang up.

"Mike?"

"What?"

"I'm glad you called," she said. "Sleep tight."

I sat there a long time, feet on the coffee table, swimming in my desire for her. But powerful as that feeling was, it could not stand up to self-doubt. I could convince myself that, now, at this stage of my life, I could remain faithful to her, rationalize that I could never grow tired of her. But the truth stood there like a boulder in my gut. *You still have the urges of an alley cat.*

And there was another truth. My days were bound together by the hope of another chance, of a life with her again someday. But what if I brought her my undying commitment, and she shot me down? How then would I get through the next, single hour?

It was Stapler's groan that brought me out of that. He was sitting in the middle of the room with his leash in his jaws, ears cocked toward me. He whined again, thumped his tail, trotted over and raked a nail across my knee.

"Okay, buddy, let's go out," I said, and I took him for a walk, feeling better in the brace of night air, savoring the intimacy of her final words: *sleep tight.*

I turned the corner onto Leavitt, the light down at Armitage changing to green, and forced myself to consider the meager facts of the Ambertoe case. There was a hyena loose in Humboldt Park; those guys in the pickup truck were trying to capture it; and David Akibu, who was at the abandoned building around the time Reggie Brockton disappeared, dealt in African animal skins. Sure it was a stretch. But what else was there?

Marty said the men in the pickup were staying at Fiftieth on the Lake, an Outer Drive motel on the shore of Lake Michigan. Tomorrow happened to be September 21st, the autumnal equinox—what better day to watch the sun hoist itself out of the lake and split the world perfectly in two?

Marty had asked me if I didn't have anything better to do. *No Marty, I don't.*

CHAPTER EIGHT

Next morning I drove south on Lake Shore Drive in darkness, Stapler standing on the back seat, his nose out the window into the wind off the lake. I pulled into the motel parking lot and saw the red pickup with the Texas plates nosed against the wall.

I backed into a spot across the aisle and several spaces down, and settled in to wait. Dawn crept in, its somber glow barely noticeable at first. Then a spot at the edge of the earth, exactly on the east point of the compass, began to pinken. It turned to orange, burning brighter and brighter, and now the top of the sun lifted up and spread itself on the horizon like an egg sizzling in a frying pan. Now the yolk rose higher, then higher, until finally it let go of the earth and the sun pulled itself into a perfectly round, red ball.

And then I saw the two men come out of the motel and walk toward the truck, a tall one with a pearl-colored cowboy hat, a shorter, stocky one with the same kind of hat, only black. They wore Levis and cowboy boots, the short one in a blue denim jacket, the tall one in a tan Carhart, both with their collars turned up. When Stapler saw them he jumped into the front seat, stood with his paws on the dashboard and pumped his tail. I opened the door and let him out. He trotted over to them, stood shamelessly begging for attention as the tall one opened the door of the truck.

"Well, looky here," the tall one said, hunkering down. He scratched Stapler behind the ears, then lifted his eyes to me as I walked over to them, his rawhide face sculpted by sun and wind. "That is one fine-looking dog."

"Llewellyn, isn't he?" asked the other.

I nodded. "You know your dogs," I said.

"Bird dogs, I do. How is he on birds?"

"Got a great nose," I said. "If there's a bird in the county, Stapler will find it. But he's not so good at holding point. Likes to bust birds just before I get ready to shoot."

They both laughed. "Stapler, huh?" said the tall one, now massaging the dog's scalp. "Bet there's a story in that name."

"Sort of."

"Kind of thought so. Probably he just needs a little seasoning. You know Elmer here, he's an honest-to-God dog trainer. You ought to see what he can do with a dog."

"What kind of birds do y'all hunt around here?" Elmer asked.

"Grouse and woodcock, mostly. But not around here. 'Way up north, Wisconsin and Minnesota. Illinois isn't much of a place for upland birds."

"Well, can't say I've hunted grouse much. Woodcock, neither, they ain't none in Texas."

"But we shoot a lot of chukar partridge and quail, and sharp tails," said the tall one. "Elmer and I do some guiding. It's a lot different, though, than hunting grouse. We use English pointers, real rangy dogs. With quail, we follow 'em on horseback. That dog of yours hunt close?"

"Not as close as he should," I said. "But I keep hoping he'll get better."

"Nate Wilcox," the tall one said, extending a hand. It felt like granite closing around mine. "This is Elmer Bumpp. No kidding, Elmer really is a world-class dog trainer. Rich folks from all over the country ship their dogs down to Elmer. I always say Elmer gets along so good with dogs on account of their IQs are about equal."

Elmer chuckled, smiled over at me, but didn't say anything.

"Sounds like you might be exactly what Stapler needs," I said to him. "How long do you generally keep a dog?"

"It varies, depending on how much the dog needs. And what the owner wants. Minimum a week, up to a month or more."

"Why don't you give him one of your cards," Nate said.

Elmer dug through his wallet, handed me a business card, bent and a little soiled. "Sorry, it's my last one. Didn't catch your name," he said, extending a hand.

"Mike Duncavan." I shook his hand, glancing at the card: Live Oak Kennels, Meltrey, Texas.

"We was just heading into breakfast, Mike. Care to join us?"

"Sure," I said. "Just let me put Stapler in the car."

We went in, and as we made our way to a booth, Elmer said, "Okay, so how'd you name your Llewellyn?"

"I don't have a lot of imagination," I said. "He went nameless for a long time, until a friend suggested that I just sit down, close my eyes, clear my head of everything, then call him the first thing pops into my mind. Unfortunately, I was sitting at my desk at the time."

Elmer laughed, but Nate gave his head an empathetic shake. I wasn't sure if the empathy was intended for me or the dog. "Coulda been a lot worse."

We ate breakfast talking of shotguns and dogs and upland bird shooting. I had hoped they would mention Mesquite Bend Ranch, but when we finished and the waitress brought the check and they still hadn't mentioned it, I tried a subtle nudge. "You guys ever hunt big game?"

"Sure," said Nate. "Matter of fact, I used to guide elk up in Idaho. I still take a bull every year, mostly for freezer meat."

"Nate's from up that way," said Elmer. "I'm a Texan through and through. I've shot elk, but all that humping up and down the mountains just ain't my cup of tea. I've shot a mule deer every season since I was nine years old, though. And Texas, you know, is prime turkey country. I guide turkey hunters every year, too. Ever hunted turkeys?"

I shook my head.

"You ought to come down, try it, Mike. The turkey is the absolute king of game birds."

I thought of another angle. "I always thought that some day, if I ever had enough money, I'd like to do an African safari. Don't think it's going to happen, though."

They both nodded. No bites.

"What do you do down there, Nate, when you're not guiding?" I said.

"We both work for a game ranch."

"Oh?" I said, "which one?"

If the question seemed lame, they showed no reaction. "Mesquite Bend," Nate said, "you probably never heard of it."

Since I was a hunter, it didn't seem too out of the ordinary that I would have. "Sure I've heard of it," I said. "That's where you can shoot African antelope, right?"

Nate nodded, his expression unchanged. "That's the place," he said. But Elmer suddenly looked serious, his eyes narrowing a little.

"How does that work?" I asked. "As a hunting experience, I mean. Is it like stalking wild animals?"

"I really can't say," Nate said. "We aren't involved in that end of it much. To each his own, I guess."

"So," I said. "What brings you guys to Chicago, anyway?"

Elmer was frowning now, studying the back of his hands.

"Oh, just some ranch business," Nate said.

Elmer squirmed, then jerked his wrist from the table, looked at his watch. "Balls, look at the time. We'd best be going."

"I got this," I said, and picked up the check. "What sort of business?"

Elmer looked at me directly. "The man told you. Ranch business."

I decided to put all my chips on one number and let the wheel spin. "Would you maybe have brought a pair of hyenas up here?"

Elmer guffawed, his face turning red. But Nate's expression never changed, and neither did his tone. His eyes were clear as gun metal and deeply creased at the corners, eyes made for open spaces, for spotting things on the horizon. "What sort of work do you do, Mike?" he asked.

"Here's how I see it. You've got two dog kennels in the back of the truck, but no dogs. You've been seen in Humboldt Park. There's a hyena loose in Humboldt Park . . ."

"Huh!" said Elmer. "Say, what the hay-ull are you talking about?"

Nate touched the back of Elmer's hand to silence him.

"Trust me," I said. "There's a hyena loose in Humboldt Park. But then, you guys know that, because you were trying to catch it, get it back."

Elmer flushed. "Listen, Mister . . ."

Nate touched his hand again, then looked at me. "Go on, Mike."

I held his eye. "I figure you came up here to deliver two hyenas, but one got away somehow. You must have deliv-

ered the other one to somebody. Now I don't know anything about importing animals like that, but I'm sure you
fellas do, working at that ranch. And I'd guess what you're
doing violates the law. I just want to know who you delivered the other one to."

"And I get the feeling you ain't a cop, or you would have
dropped some identification on us by now. So what's your
interest here, Mike?"

I shrugged. "I walk my dog in that park. I don't want
him eaten by a hyena. Is that interest enough?"

"No," Nate said, and with a cocked wrist he thrust his
hand across the table, shook my hand. "But thanks for
breakfast."

Elmer didn't offer to shake hands. The two of them got
up, Nate's friendly smile never changing, Elmer avoiding
eye contact. I took two cards from my wallet, gave one to
each of them. "You guys ever want to talk about this, give
me a call. Collect."

Nate looked at the card and stuck it in his shirt pocket,
still smiling. Elmer's eye went from the card to me. "Shee-
it," he said.

As they walked away I noticed for the first time how
worn their cowboy boots were. After they disappeared out
the door I waited, giving them a chance to get away. I actually liked those guys.

CHAPTER NINE

I headed back north on Lake Shore Drive at slug speed in rush hour traffic, and dropped Stapler at home. I didn't get to the office until after eleven, wishing there was someone I could bill for the wasted morning. I sure couldn't bill it to Ambertoe's case.

I brewed a pot of coffee and sat with a mug, my chair turned to the window, watching the foot traffic across Washington Street, wishing I knew just what the cops had unearthed about Reggie Brockton's disappearance, what more they might have on Ambertoe. Or what they thought they had. Trouble was, they were focused on him now, looking for evidence to prove him guilty, which meant they were not looking for anyone else. Had they charged Ambertoe, we'd at least have a small advantage: they'd have to turn everything they knew over to us. Stan Janda could at least get a look at all their cards.

Ambertoe's hesitancy, when I told him what Bonnerly had said about his talking to the African, was troubling me. But then Ambertoe wasn't real comfortable with me anyway. I had to be careful not to misjudge him. The cops were doing a great job of that.

The phone rang. I spun my chair away from the window and snatched it up before the second ring. "Legal Investigations."

Whoever it was seemed to be thought-gathering for a couple of seconds, and then a woman's voice said, "May I

65

speak to Mr. Mike Duncavan?" Elderly. She liked to enunciate her words.

"This is Mike."

"Mr. Duncavan, this is Julia Ambertoe. Justin's mother? Did I reach you at a bad time?"

"This is a good time," I said, curious.

More thought gathering. "I don't know how to say this," she said.

"I'm not going anywhere, Mrs. Ambertoe. Take your time."

"I know that you're trying to help Justin. He's an only child, you know. His father's deceased. He's all I've got in the world. I just want you to know that . . . that I have means. Please, I wouldn't want anything left undone because . . . do you understand my meaning? If there is anything you feel you need to do—anything—I want you to do it. You will be compensated."

"Mrs. Ambertoe, you should really be talking to his lawyer, Stanley Janda. My contract is with him."

"I just got off the phone with Mr. Janda, and told him the same thing. But he said that until Justin has been formally charged, there was little he could do. He used that word, *formally,* as if it were inevitable, an accomplished fact." She paused; I waited.

"Mr. Janda told me that, if anyone in the world can help him now, it is you. He spoke most highly of you, Mr. Duncavan. I am aware that you send your bills to him. But I asked him if it would be all right if I spoke to you personally. He said that would be fine."

"I'll do everything I can, Mrs. Ambertoe."

"I detest the expression, 'Spare no expense,' but please, whatever your bill is, be assured it will be paid."

"Can I make it retroactive?" I asked.

That hesitation again. "I'm afraid I don't understand."

"Nothing. A joke," I said.

"Oh," she said. "Good one, Mr. Duncavan. Please pardon me if I seem not in the mood for humor."

"Sorry. Look, I really would like to know more about Justin. What can you tell me about him?"

"What can I tell you? I'm his mother, what would you like to know? He's an extremely gentle person, always was, even as a child. Perhaps too gentle—at least his father thought so. Other children picked on him, tended to bully him. He would never fight back, not even verbally. Maybe it would have been better if he had. I know he carries terrible wounds. His father . . . I don't even know how to tell you, but there is no possibility that Justin could hurt any living thing, let alone a child. I know those are the words of a mother, but they are absolutely true."

"What were you going to say about his father?" I turned my chair back to the window and put my feet on the sill, waiting for a tale of yet another misunderstood child. The traffic light on Washington Street turned red. A man with a walker started from the curb. He was nearly halfway across when she spoke.

"I don't know how to say it," she said.

"Was it that your husband never understood Justin?"

"No. In fact, something of the opposite. Justin is one of those people blinded by their own suffering. It was really Justin who never understood his father. Never gave him a chance." She paused again. "It feels strange telling you this."

"And I don't mean to pry. But the more I can learn about Justin, the more I can help him."

"It's quite all right, I want to tell you everything I can. It's just hard, over the telephone." Another pause. "Justin believed that his father never loved him, while in fact his father loved him more than life itself. He was just a man who found it hard to express his feelings, to show affection, especially toward his own son. Howard was in the oil business, very much a self-made man. He started out in the oil fields as a roughneck when he was just a teenager, then got a night school degree in geology. He was a driven man. When Justin was small, Howard was never around. He spent his life regretting that fact, died regretting it. He would have given back all his wealth, everything, if he could have changed that."

"Did he tell you that?"

"More than once."

"But he was never able to tell that to Justin, was he?"

"I think you understand the situation, Mr. Duncavan. Quite sad."

That night after dinner, as I sat watching television, Fred Habranek, my landlord, came to the door.

"I can't stay, Mike," he said, standing in the middle of the living room. He removed his baseball cap, exposing a shiny cranium and a laurel leaf of salt-and-pepper hair. "I'm catching a flight to Los Angeles in the morning. My brother's in a bad way. It's the big C. I don't think he's got much time left."

"I'm sorry, Fred. Anything I can do?"

"I wanted to ask a favor." He squatted down and, scratching Stapler behind the ears, said, "Could you look after Butler while I'm gone? He's no trouble; he's got a clean litter box. He likes to be let out at night, but you'll find him hanging around the back door in the morning, wanting to be fed." He hesitated. "Thing is, I'm not sure how long I'll be gone. I'm figuring about a week, but it could be longer."

"No problem," I said. Butler was a pretty independent cat. He and Stapler went to great lengths to ignore each other. "I'd be glad to do it."

"There's a big bag of Friskies on the kitchen table. Just put about half a cup in his bowl. And if you wouldn't mind filling his water bowl." He handed me a key to his apartment. "I'll call you when I know more."

As he was going out the door, I asked him, "You need a ride to the airport?"

He shook his head and smiled. "Thanks, Mike, I got someone to drive me."

"Well, if you need to be picked up when you get back, just give me a call."

CHAPTER TEN

I overslept the following morning, and by the time I finished with the weights and the speed bag and the heavy bag, it was nearly eight o'clock. I skipped my morning coffee, jumped in the shower and stuffed the *Sun-Times* into my briefcase as I went out to the car.

At the office there were two messages waiting on the answering machine. The first was from Mrs. Overhill, the African guy's former landlady, asking me to call. The other was from Stan Janda.

Luckily, Mrs. Overhill was in. "I talked to one of my other tenants about Kimberly Price," she said. "The man had loaned Kim some money, and so he had her address." She gave it to me, West Grace Street, on the north side. I thanked her.

Stan Janda's message was only two words: "Call me." His tone was grim. I dialed his number, and when his secretary connected me, he didn't even say hello. "Did you see the morning paper?"

"Not yet."

"There's another kid missing in Englewood," he said. "The police picked up Justin Ambertoe again."

"Did they book him?"

"No, they advised him of his rights, and tried to grill him, but he was smart enough this time not to say anything, other than he wanted to call his lawyer. They didn't let him call me, but they didn't really question him after that, either. They held him about two hours and let him go."

"Do you know anything about the missing kid?"

"There was just a short article. It was a little girl this time, a little older than Reggie Brockton. Eight, I think it says. She went out on her bicycle after dinner, never came back."

"They find the bike?"

"It doesn't say." He thought a second. "The police could be holding back on that."

"How's Justin taking it?"

"He's pretty shook up. I feel bad for him." A pause. "How're things going on your end? Anything at all?"

"No," I said. I told him what I'd gleaned from Bonnerly, the guy who lived across the street from the abandoned building. "I don't know what to make of it. Even if he exaggerated about how long he saw Justin talking to this African, the stories are still at odds. I mean, it was either a momentary meeting or it wasn't. I really want to talk to this guy, a David Akibu, if I can find him."

"You think he's involved?"

"Just a hunch. But, look at it this way. Both he and Justin are seen hanging around the abandoned building. Yet no one suspects him, because he lives in the neighborhood."

"And Justin sticks out like a sore thumb. Kind of racial profiling in reverse."

"Nothing reverse about it." And, I thought: *nothing really wrong with it, either. Why shouldn't the cops focus on Ambertoe?*

Janda's mind was running in the same channel. "Yeah, but face it. If you were the homicide dick, what would you do?"

"I'd be on Ambertoe's ass like flies on a turd."

"Damn straight you would. And we can't forget that the

African wasn't seen *inside* the building, like Justin was. And his fingerprints aren't on the kid's scooter."

"We don't know that. I've got a hunch they are," I said.

I hung up, knowing that my hunch was a colossal leap. But a hunch to an investigator is like a pipe wrench to a plumber. Especially when it's all you've got.

I put on a pot of coffee and retrieved the newspaper from my briefcase, found the article about the missing little girl. Her name was Lawanda Henry, eight years old, living about a mile from Reggie Brockton's house. Lawanda went for a bike ride after dinner and never came back.

I went home and fed Stapler; then after dinner I drove to the Grace Street address to interview Kimberly Price, figuring it was the best chance to find her at home. Kimberly lived in a three-flat building on the corner, her name Scotch-taped above a doorbell. I rang it. Half a minute later, a voice I assumed was hers came over the intercom: "Who is it?"

"My name's Mike Duncavan, ma'am. I'm a private investigator. Can I talk to you for just a minute?"

"What about?"

"David Akibu."

"David? What, has something happened to David?" Before I could answer, she said, "Wait, I'll be right down."

I heard her footsteps coming quickly down the staircase, and then she came into view, framed in the glass of the door. She opened it just wide enough to talk through and, before I could say anything, she repeated: "Has something happened to David?"

She was nicely put together, a shade on the voluptuous side, pretty green eyes. She wore black pedal pushers and, although only the top two buttons of her white blouse were open, she still showed considerable cleavage. Her skin, like the streaks in her hair, was the color of honey.

"No, no, nothing like that. I just need to talk to him."

"You're a policeman? What do you want to talk to him about?"

"No, ma'am, I'm a private investigator. Can you tell me how I can reach him?"

"That depends. What do you want him for?"

"You lived in the same rooming house with him, on Stewart?"

"That's right." Her tone was guarded.

"There was a boy who disappeared in that neighborhood, after you moved out. Reggie Brockton. And we're trying . . ."

Her voice rose. "And you think David had something to do with *that*?"

"No, I just want to talk to anyone who . . ."

"I know about the missing boy, I read the newspapers. Who do you work for, Mister . . . ?"

"Duncavan. Mike Duncavan. Actually, I'm working with the lawyer for Justin Ambertoe."

Her eyes flicked sideways, searching for where she'd heard the name, then joined mine again. "You mean you're working for the man who kidnapped the boy? And you want me to *help* you?" Her face drew itself into a cold smile.

"He didn't kidnap the boy," I said. "The police haven't charged him with that; he's only a suspect. Look, I need to talk to Mr. Akibu. Any little piece of information could help." Help who, I didn't say. But I didn't have to, she knew.

She was shaking her head slowly, drilling me with her eyes; then, without another word, she cast her eyes down and pulled the door shut. Through the glass I watched her ascend the stairs until she disappeared around the corner, never looking back.

I took a card from my wallet, started to drop it into the mail slot. I drew it back and, in what could only have been a sign of desperation, I did something I never do: I jotted my home phone number on the back. Then I dropped it inside. You just never know.

That night I was in my bathrobe and slippers, enjoying a Stoli on the rocks and watching the evening news, when a shocker of a story hit me like a bucket of cold water. The body of Reggie Brockton had been found in a Dumpster behind a Jewel Food Store in Englewood. The body had been mutilated: the liver, the kidneys, the heart had been cut out.

It took a long time to get to sleep that night. Mutilation—what the hell were we dealing with here?

The next morning I was so preoccupied with the discovery of Reggie's body that I almost forgot to feed Butler before I left for the office. I went down the back stairs, found the little guy pacing the first-floor landing at Fred's back door. I let us both in, poured Friskies in his bowl, replenished his water dish, then locked the door behind me.

I turned eastbound onto Armitage, dialing Stan Janda on my cell phone, hoping he hadn't left for court or something. Luckily, he was in the office. He'd already heard the news about Reggie Brockton's body.

"Do you know any more than what's in the newspapers?" I asked.

"I heard they found traces of semen on the body. They're running DNA tests."

"That's good for us," I said. "Excellent."

"I was thinking the same thing," he said, but there was

no cheer in his voice. The time for relief would come after the test results came back.

I hung up, the weight of unanswered questions pressing me into the seat. The body had been mutilated, the organs cut out. What was the killer's motive? Just how precisely did he remove the organs? This was more than a random act of violence.

The burden stayed with me through the rest of the day, and when I got home that evening the message light on the answering machine was flashing. It was a message from my sister, Helen, the weary resignation in her voice adding to the weight on my shoulders. "I'm afraid I'm calling with some bad news, Mike. Please call me."

CHAPTER ELEVEN

I didn't talk to my sister as often as I should have. For her own part, she rarely called me unless she was delivering bad news. I called her back, heart already heavy, knowing what it must be about. Our mother, who had been in a nursing home for the past four years, was gone at ninety-seven. For the last few months, we were expecting her to go any day. Though truth was, Mom had already left us, had departed bit by bit until all that was left was that hollow shell devoid of mind and memory.

"I think we should have a wake, Mike," she said.

"Helen, there's no one left who knew her. It would be pointless."

"It's what we do, Mike; it's the civilized thing to do. She would have wanted it. Pa would have wanted it. Don't worry about a thing. I'll make the arrangements, okay?"

"Thanks, Helen."

She said goodbye and was about to hang up when she said, "Oh, I already called Beth. She thinks the wake is a good idea."

Beth. Helen still thought of my ex as family, and that notion was an inexpressible comfort. "Thank you, Helen," I said.

I put on my pajamas, went down the back stairs to Fred's apartment and, instead of letting Butler out, brought him back up with me. He sat on my lap in my living room chair, his motor purring away while I stroked his back. Stapler curled at my feet with his cold nose against my bare ankle. I wondered if it was true that Eskimos of old left their elderly behind in the snow to freeze to death. Barbaric, of course. Cruel—but to whom? I've heard that freezing is a peaceful way to go; they say you just fall asleep. We, on the other hand, warehouse our elderly and wait for them to die. Whose sensibilities are we protecting? It is as though, at our late stage of evolution, we need to deny our mortality.

I took Butler to the back door and released him into the night, and he seemed happy to go. Then I let Stapler out in the yard for a while, and when he came back up I went to bed.

At the office the following day, I was feeling even lower than I'd expected I would. The only person I called to tell about Mom's death was Marty Richter—he was the only one I could think of who knew her. Marty and I had gone to the same parish school together.

Kerrigan's Funeral Home was on the south side, on Seventy-ninth Street near Pulaski. I went in, stood a moment in the doorway to the funeral parlor, the expanse of unfilled chairs underscoring the emptiness. There were three people there, a man I did not recognize from behind, sitting near the back, and Helen with another woman in the front row, both of them dressed in black. As I approached up the side aisle, I saw that the other woman was Beth, and my heart turned over with joy.

Beth stood when she saw me, and before I could speak she put her arms around my neck and kissed my cheek. "I'm so sorry, Mike," she said. "She was one of my all-time favorites, you know."

I hugged my sister then, greeted her with more gratitude

than she would understand. She'd made all the arrangements, asking for no help from me. But most of all, she brought Beth here.

I was about to kneel at the casket to say a prayer when Beth gestured with her head toward the back, to the man sitting there. In the last row, eyes cast down, sat Justin Ambertoe. I walked back to him.

"I'm very sorry, Mike," he said, getting to his feet. "Mr. Janda told me."

No more than twenty people showed up during the entire evening. Marty Richter dropped in, drove over from the station in uniform. "Donna's coming later," he said.

His wife Donna did, about an hour later. After paying her respects, Donna and Beth went down to the kitchen for coffee. They were gone a long time. When they returned, Donna sat quietly for a while, and when she got up to leave, I told her I would walk her to her car.

"It is so nice to see you and Beth together again," she said as we walked.

"We aren't exactly together."

"I know, I just mean . . ." Her voice trailed off as though she abandoned that thought. She pressed the remote to unlock her car door, then lifted her eyes into mine. "Mike, she's not going to wait for you forever."

"Wait? She's not . . . I'm not sure what you mean," I said.

She stared at me as if trying to get a look at something behind my eyes. "Mike . . ." she said. Then, "Never mind."

I went back and sat with the two women. No one else came after Donna left, and when it was time to go, Justin was still sitting there alone.

The four of us walked out together, and in the parking lot Beth turned to me. "Mike, I'm hungry, I think you should buy us all dinner."

"Good idea." Of course I meant it—anything to keep Beth close a little longer. I dreaded saying good night to her, dreaded watching her drive off.

"Thanks, but I'm exhausted," Helen said, and I could see that she was. She kissed me on the cheek, and the three of us waited there until she drove off.

We drove together to The Old Barn, my favorite south side restaurant, in Beth's car. We found a corner booth with a candle on the table, and Justin sat on one side, Beth and I on the other. Beth sat close, her thigh sometimes pressing against mine, and she touched my arm frequently. It was easy to pretend that the life we once had together had never broken apart; sadness touched me only in the moments I realized the evening would end.

Beth and Justin, the two artists, hit it off. We sat there a long time and we drank a lot, all three of us. I didn't say much, just sat on the sidelines with only an occasional comment, and basked in the glow of their conversation. They talked eagerly of their respective forms, and I took delight in watching the shimmer of Beth's eyes. I thought I could feel the warmth of her body glowing against mine.

When the conversation turned to the commercial aspects of their work, Beth was self-effacing. "I guess you could describe my work as 'kitschy,' " she said.

"Don't believe it," I said.

Justin shrugged. "One man's kitsch . . ." He stifled a giggle, and let that thought die. "Funny, in my own work, what I like best is the stuff that no one wants to buy. That's the stuff I do just for myself."

"Do you have pieces, like I do, that are just not for sale?"

He shook his head. "I wouldn't go that far—it's all for sale. There's just not much market for black-and-whites these days, but it's the black-and-whites that have all the power for me, the subtlety."

There was a quiet moment then. Justin sipped his wine, then said, "It's hard to imagine you two are—" He made an ambiguous gesture with his hand.

"Divorced?" Beth said. "It's okay, you can say it." She slipped her arm through mine, took my hand. "Actually he's the only man I've ever loved—at least so far." It was probably the wine that was calling out her surprising frankness. "But someday a new prince will come." Then she smiled impishly, picked up her wineglass, sipped, put it down and made a circle with its base on the tablecloth. "But Mike's heart has way too much love for just one woman. Right, Mike?"

"Beth, let's not," I said.

"Okay." The wine was definitely loosening her tongue. "Also, Mike has a rather impulsive nature." She gave it a beat. "An impulsive *and* violent nature."

"Beth, come on. He'll think I beat you or something."

She was taking another sip and she moved the glass from her mouth too quickly. "M-m-m, sorry." She patted her lips. "No, no, Mike is a really gentle person. He only beats up bad guys."

"Thanks," I said. "Do you think we could change the subject?"

"And an occasional judge." Now she giggled.

"Beth, could you . . ."

"Okay, okay, lighten up, Mike." She turned her eyes to mine, squeezed my arm and smiled as if, inside her head, she was seeing some better time. "Mike is—he's one of a

80

kind, Justin. Sort of untamed. He's got one foot in one kind of world, the other in another. One world is a little on the primitive side. That puts him a little off-balance some-times."

"I'm unbalanced. Now there's a compliment."

Justin laughed.

"I mean it in a good way." She patted my arm.

Justin laughed again.

"I wouldn't have him any other way." She turned her gaze to me and grinned. "Evolution's not all it's cracked up to be, Mike." Her eyes, shiny with candlelight, stayed on mine, and her smile drifted away, and for a moment I thought she was going to kiss me. But Justin was sitting there, so I knew she wouldn't.

Then, Justin or not, I fought back my own urge to kiss her and was losing the battle when she must have seen it coming and took her eyes away. She picked up her glass, swirled the wine and sat back. "What about you, Justin? Is there a significant other in your life?"

"There is," he said. "I've been in a committed relation-ship for eight years now."

"Come on, tell us about it," she said, "it's your turn." She waited for an answer, her lips parted expectantly. In the silence I heard the air-conditioning motor come on.

"Richard has AIDS," he said frankly. "I'm afraid he doesn't have much longer."

Beth put her fingers on the back of his hand, held them there. "I'm sorry."

His eyes started to glisten. "It's been . . ." He looked away, his eyes going out of focus. Then he looked at Beth. "Richard needs a lot of care. Fortunately, I'm self-employed, so I can spend a lot of time with him. I wish I could be there twenty-four hours, but I can't. I mean—how can I say this? I can't emotionally. I know it sounds terrible, but I need to get away now and then. I feel awful saying it. I know there will come a day when knowing I could have spent more time with him will be unbearable." He looked away again, then down at the table and brushed at his eye with his wrist. "I should be there now. He's all alone."

Beth reached over, cupped her hand on his cheek. "He loves you, Justin. You love him. And I know he understands. There will come a day when you'll just treasure what you've given to each other. When you'll be grateful for that time you did spend with him."

Beth drove us back to the funeral home, pulled into the parking lot and, as she sat with the motor running, Justin said good night and got out without delay, believing, perhaps, that I was about to get lucky. If so, he didn't know Beth. But I did have some hope of my own.

"Are you all right to drive?" I asked, wishing she'd turn off the ignition.

"I'll be fine." Her eyes searched mine. "Mike, you weren't insulted back there, were you? When I said evolution's not all it's cracked up to be? I like to kid you. Sometimes I think I go too far."

"Not even a little," I said.

"Thing is, I mean it. Your best traits seem to have been bred out of most men. Honesty and courage don't seem to come naturally to anyone anymore. Now, men just want to show you they can cry. I don't know why they think that's so wonderful. And here you are, Mike . . ." She gave me a smile that signaled a punchline was on the way. "A guy that makes other men cry."

"Full of compliments tonight," I said.

"Seriously, I sometimes think that if men like you

headed these huge corporations, there could never be scandals like Enron and Worldcom."

"It's a long drive to Sutler's Grove," I said. "Why not spend the night at my place?"

She put her head back and laughed freely. "Now there's a seamless segue." Then she moved her eyes into mine, still smiling but slowly shaking her head, and gave my hand a squeeze.

"No, really," I said, "no funny stuff. I'll sleep on the couch."

She just kept looking at me and shaking her head that way, a smile of disbelief in her eyes. Then she turned to look through the windshield. "Tell you what, Mike." I waited. She seemed to be deciding something. "We're having an art fair in Sutler's Grove, week after next. Last year it was just for the residents, just for everyone to show their stuff to the neighbors. It was more like a big block party, but this year we decided to invite other exhibitors, too. It's going to be pretty big. How about coming out, giving me a hand? I'll need some help, and it'll be fun."

"Just exactly what sort of fun are you promising?"

She laughed again. "Not that kind. But it would still be nice if you came."

"Sure, I'll be there."

"Great, I'll put a flyer in the mail." She was looking into my eyes again, her smile more relaxed now, and then she leaned to kiss my cheek. I turned, caught her lips, pulled her to me and kissed her deeply. For a moment she didn't resist, then she pulled her face away. "Devil," she said. "Good night."

I got into my car and waited while she pulled out, sat there watching her tail lights move down Seventy-ninth Street and disappear.

I drove home bubbling with delight. She'd invited me to the art fair, remembering as I had a thousand times before that she'd been the greatest thing in my life, and I'd blown it.

No, maybe I was still blowing it. Maybe I shouldn't have let her drive off, maybe I should have begged her to take me back, now, this night. But women once were my addiction. How did I know it was ended, that this time I could remain faithful to her?

Or worse: what if her answer was no? A flat-out, final no?

When I got home, there was a message from Fred Habranek on my answering machine.

"Mike, I'm sorry, I'm afraid I just don't know how long I'll be staying. My brother's in a bad way, but hanging on. I'll keep you posted." He paused and, sounding a little embarrassed, added, "There's, um, a bag of kitty litter on the floor of the pantry. I hope you don't mind. Call if you need to talk to me."

He left a phone number, but I didn't call him back. I went downstairs, let Butler out and changed his litter box.

CHAPTER TWELVE

Two weeks later, I took Stapler for a long walk after dinner, one of those crisp fall evenings when the tree shadows on the sidewalk are noticeably thinner and fallen leaves crackle underfoot, and a fresh chill sweetens the air. I was hanging my jacket in the front closet when I got back, and the phone rang.

"Mr. Duncavan?" A woman, a voice I didn't recognize, was whispering into the phone.

"This is Mike," I said, slipping off Stapler's leash.

"It's Kim Price; I have to talk to you," she said, a tremor in her voice. It took a couple of seconds to remember who she was: the cosmetologist friend of David Akibu.

"Can you meet me somewhere. *Please?*"

"You mean now?"

"Yes, *please,* it's really important."

"Can you give me some idea what it's . . ."

"It's about David Akibu," she hissed, trying not to be heard by whoever was there. Then she didn't say anything for ten seconds, and I got the idea she was weeping. When she spoke again her tone, still kept low, was more angry than frightened. "I don't know how to tell you. He's evil. He's an evil, evil man. Will you meet me somewhere, please?"

"Sure, where?"

"Do you know the Green Mill, on Broadway?"

"Yeah. I can be there in maybe half an hour. But listen, are you in some kind of danger?"

"No." She hesitated. Then, "Yes, I am." She stifled a sob. "Please, the Green Mill."

"Look, if you're in danger, call the police."

"I can't."

"I'll call them; tell me where you are."

"No, I don't need the police, I need to talk to you. God, do you know anything about him?" Her voice quavered. "He's involved with . . . Moody," she said, the last word crackling into a falsetto.

"Did you say 'Moody'?"

"Moody, Moody, yes!"

"But I don't . . . who's Moody?"

There was the sound of a man's voice in the background, abrupt, angry words; then her own voice away from the phone shouted something unintelligible; then: "I don't *care!*"

"Here, give it to me," I heard the man order, and then he was speaking to me.

"Mistah Duncavan? This is David Akibu. I understand you want to find me. That would be very bad for you, Mistah Duncavan. You do not want to find me. I assure you that would be the worst thing that ever could happen to you." He spoke in a baritone, self-possessed, mesmerizing.

"All the same, I'd really like to talk to you," I said. "Even more so, now. But for the moment, put Kim back on, will you?"

"Do you know what pain is, Mr. Duncavan? I don't think you do, not the pain that is truly exquisite. It is pain which you cannot even imagine. No, you do not want to find me."

"Put Kim on," I said.

"I will give you this one opportunity. Do not try to find me. It is your only hope."

"David," I said. "Mind if I call you David? David, ever hear of a guy named Marcus Garvey? He had a movement a long time ago in Chicago, called the Back to Africa Movement. Nothing ever came of it, but it might be just the thing for an obnoxious shit like you. Give it some thought, okay? Now put Kim back on."

His laugh was like the belching of a volcano. "You want to find me, Mistah Duncavan? Very well, then. I will find you, how is that? Now listen to me. Listen very carefully. Are you listening?" His voice had changed somehow, his words slower, measured, the rhythm disarming. "Tonight, I will come into your head as you sleep. Tonight you will dream of David Akibu. And it will not be pleasant, Mistah Duncavan."

"Listen, you lowlife fuck, put Kim back on."

"Pleasant dreams, Mistah Duncavan." He gave that laugh again, deep and lingering, and I heard the connection break, and then the dial tone.

I considered calling the police, but he hadn't threatened her, nor had he threatened me, not physically, and I heard no sounds of violence. And she said herself she didn't want the police.

Driving to the Green Mill, my head kept reverberating with the drumbeat of his words, like a song you can't get rid of, only this was seriously discomfiting. I didn't like the effect it was having on me. There was no reason to be afraid of this shit, and yet . . . it was giving me an unsettling feeling that I couldn't shake. An ache rose out of my belly, the kind you get when worry takes hold of you, but I couldn't think of anything I should be worrying about.

Less than forty minutes after I'd hung up, I was paying the cover charge to the guy at the door of the Green Mill, it being open mike poetry night. The place was packed. I squeezed along the bar, scanning the crowd, and worked all the way to the back. She was not at the bar, not in any of the booths and not at any of the tables in front of the stage. I couldn't find an empty stool, so I wedged myself into a spot at the bar where I could keep an eye on the door.

Four bad poets and two double Stolis later, she still hadn't showed. I thought of ordering another, but didn't. I listened to one more anguished soul at the microphone and left, drove to her building and stood on the sidewalk looking up at the dark windows of her apartment. No sign of light or movement. Then I rang the bell. No answer. Maybe she'd had too much to drink. Maybe it was a lover's quarrel, and they'd patched things up. Maybe they were all cuddly and stuck together and humping up there right now.

But . . . ?

Driving home, I thought again about Akibu's you-don't-want-to-find-me bullshit, the words ringing in my head, and I turned on WFMT. They were playing Wagner and I turned it up, hoping to drown out that baritone which seemed to wrap itself around my brain like a squid. *I will come into your head tonight, Mistah Duncavan.*

Back home, I poured three fingers of Stoli over ice, went to the computer and did a Google search on "Moody." The hit list was endless. The Moody Bible Institute, which had more offspring than I ever knew: Moody Radio, Moody Books, Moody Aviation, *Moody Bible Magazine.* There was also The Moody Blues, Moody Investment Services, Moody Bank, Moody Air Force Base. A place in Florida called Moody Gardens, and lots of interesting historical personages named Moody.

In two hours I searched over a hundred sites, and if any of them was a bull's eye, none of them gave me a clue.

I shut off the computer and sat at the kitchen table, the

emptiness of my apartment sucking at me like a vacuum, and wondered what Mom's parting impression of her son Mikey had been. Failed as a copper, failed as a lawyer, failed as a husband. Mom had loved Beth like she was her own daughter, and even after the divorce, they'd kept in contact.

Beth. I never wanted to lose her, not really. I just wanted to have both, my freedom and Beth, too. Now freedom encapsulated me; the empty rooms of my apartment rang with it. If I were to check out of this world tonight, how long would it take for anyone to figure out I was gone? I felt like I was stuck inside a Tom McGuane novel. McGuane said something once in an interview, something that stuck with me. Something like: "It's nice to paint your Volkswagen bus psychedelic colors and set off to find yourself. The truly sad part is the belief that everything will still be the same when you return."

Well, I had won my freedom, and there was no going back. Another word, as the song says, for nothing left to lose. I downed one more Stoli and went to bed.

The hyena came back that night. I heard it scratching at the back door first, then I heard the digging, digging, until he'd dug a hole under the door, and then its nails came ticking again, across the kitchen linoleum to the bedroom door, where it stood snuffling just out of sight. Then it craned its head around the doorjamb, black marble eyes searching for me, the eyes of a dead thing. It spotted me then, and bared its teeth and crept closer, head low, jaws dripping saliva in a guttural growl. Like the last time, I tried to get up; like the last time, I could not move. But this time it stopped short, its nails scratching the floor, struggling to come closer, but something was holding it back. Then I saw the collar around its neck, and the leash, and now into the pale frame of the doorway came David Akibu. He wore a robe of hyena skins and he grinned at me, a sliver of moonlight flashing from his teeth.

"I told you I'd come, didn't I?" The hyena whined, straining toward me. "But then, you never really doubted I'd come, did you, Mistah Duncavan?"

He put his head back and his laugh came like a mortar barrage, and then he knelt, undid the leash, and let the hyena go.

I sat straight up and jerked my feet under me, my body slippery with sweat, and I sat a minute, afraid to step off the bed. When I saw there was no hyena, I got up, flipped the light on and went through my apartment pulling open drawers, standing on a chair in the closet, reaching up on top of the china cabinet, until I found every handgun I owned. I tossed them all on the bed: a snub-nosed .357 Python, two .38 Special revolvers, the Czech 9mm, Walther .380, Browning .25, Jennings .22. I pulled down boxes of ammo from a kitchen cabinet, sat on the bed and loaded every magazine that wasn't loaded already. Then I stacked them around the bed and under my pillow and went to sleep—once more with the lights on.

The next morning I didn't go to the office. I went downstairs and fed Butler, then drove to Maxon's, the gun shop in Des Plaines. I bought ten boxes of assorted ammo and a stack of life-size silhouette targets. Although I'd never seen David Akibu, I thought they looked a lot like him, and I spent the morning shooting him full of holes until the web of my pistol hand cried out for surcease.

Later, though Kimberly Price would probably be at work, I took a chance and drove to her apartment and rang the bell. There was no answer. I rang the landlord's bell and, when she came to the door, a middle aged white woman with her hair pulled back in a bun who looked like she ate a lot of granola, I told her I was a friend of Kim's. I said that I was supposed to meet her for lunch at the beauty parlor, that I had jotted down the address but had forgotten to take it with me. It was pretty lame, but what could I lose?

"I know she works at a beauty parlor," I said. "Could you please tell me which one?"

"Well," she said hesitantly. "I don't know."

"I understand, ma'am, really, and I wouldn't even ask, but she's waiting for me, so I'm kind of stuck. Look, I'm pretty harmless-looking, wouldn't you say? Besides, it's a beauty parlor, a public place. What can go wrong? You'd be doing Kim a big favor."

"Well . . . how about if I call her, see if it's okay?"

"Good idea," I said. I still had nothing to lose.

She led me up the short flight to the first-floor apartment. "Wait here, please." I stood in the hallway while she went in, leaving the door open a little. I could hear drawers slide open, slide closed, and much shuffling of papers. When she came back she said, "I can't find where I wrote down her work number, and I don't remember the name of the place. But I guess it's okay. I don't know the exact address, but it's up there on Peterson, near Western."

I drove slowly along Peterson until I spotted what had to be the place, Magic Moments Beauty Salon in the middle of the block, and parked. Inside, a row of women sat under dryers; a couple more sat with their hands resting inside some kind of electrical box on their laps—I didn't want to know. Two hairdressers stood at chairs working on customers, neither of them Kimberly Price. One chair stood empty, as though one hairdresser was missing. It did not give me a good feeling.

Seeing me, the nearest hairdresser looked over her shoulder and yelled toward the back, "Eleanor"; then with a sly smile, her eyes slid over mine and went back to the head she was combing.

A woman in a pink uniform came out of the back. "Can I help you?"

Every head in the place was bowed, but every eye was shifted toward me. Not my most comfortable moment. "I wonder if I could see Kim Price," I said. "It'll only take a minute; I just need to tell her something."

"Sorry," she said, her lips pulling into the kind of smile you might get from sucking a lemon. "She didn't come to work today."

"Oh. I hope she's not sick," I said.

"I wouldn't know. She didn't call in."

I thanked her and left. There was nothing to do but drive downtown to my office, and I took Lake Shore Drive south toward the Loop, hoping that Kim had not come to any harm on account of me. But then, it was she who'd called me. On the other hand, she wouldn't have called me if I hadn't gone looking for her.

I was feeling pretty glum about it all, but an endless fleet of puffy cumulus was sailing the blue sky above Lake Michigan, and then Lincoln Park hove into view, regaled in a glory of fall colors, and the rarity of this fall day started putting David Akibu in a certain comic perspective. David Akibu *and* me. He'd done a nice job of planting the dream suggestion in my brain; but then, as much as I hated to admit it, he had a fertile field.

Not only had I given Akibu far too much credit, I still had nothing I could pin on him. Kimberly Price would turn up. And eventually I'd find Akibu. But then what? Well, it was too nice a day to worry about it.

CHAPTER THIRTEEN

I took Stapler for a long walk around the neighborhood at dusk, the yellow windows on the faces of the old buildings giving off the cheery light of real families gathered inside. Afterward, I drove to Kimberly Price's apartment again, and I stood for a minute on the sidewalk looking up at her windows. Again, the place was in darkness. I rang the bell anyway; no one answered.

Instead of driving back home, I drove down to the Loop, stopped at Monk's Pub, ordered a double Stoli on the rocks and carried it to a table and sat with a stenographer's notebook opened to a blank page. It stayed blank for a long time. Then I wrote "David Akibu" at the top, and then I wrote "Kim Price" under it. Then I wrote "Moody," and after that I didn't know what to write. What did I have on Akibu? Not much, except this: the bastard wanted me off his tail real bad. Why? He was guilty of something—but if I found him, then what?

As I sat mulling that over, a yuppie-looking couple came in, took a table near the door. I knew Akibu was involved with Reggie Brockton, but how was I going to prove it? His fingerprints were probably on that scooter—but how do I convince the police to look in his direction?

I had a hunch that Kim Price was the key, and a weight like a lead pig grew in my belly as the sound of her frightened voice repeated in my head. My optimism that afternoon, born of the autumn sunshine, had faded with the dying light. I had a feeling she was already dead.

And then the meager prospects of the case mingled with the meager prospects of my own life, both looking an awful lot like dead ends. I'd lost two careers and a wife, and a lot of people who used to know me pretended not to anymore. As an old copper friend used to say, some people walk through life backwards.

I signaled the bartender, ordered another Stoli and noticed, out of the corner of my eye, the male half of the couple near the door get up from the table and head my way. I looked up at him and, as his face broke into a big, boyish grin, I saw it was Blake Canavan.

I had hired Blake as a law clerk at my old firm, when he was still a law student. The firm had a human resource manager who was in charge of hiring secretaries, and a hiring committee in charge of hiring lawyers. But they put me in charge of the big decisions—the hiring of part-time law clerks.

But no one could have made a better hire than Blake. When it came to finding helpful case law, he was like a ferret in a rabbit warren. Until I'd hired him, I always preferred to do my own legal research. You had to spoon feed the clerk on all the nuances of an issue, and then you could never be sure they'd turned over every stone. But Blake was different. The best legal researcher I ever knew, he'd grab hold of a problem like a bulldog with a bone, and fairly tear up the law library. Not long after you'd brief Blake, he'd be back briefing you on all the wrinkles you'd overlooked.

During his short tenure at the firm, Blake never stopped thanking me for giving him the job. His beginnings had been as humble as my own—blue collar, south side Irish—and I was sure he'd seen his part-time job as a foot in the door with a prestigious firm. After Blake passed the bar exam, we did offer him a position, but to the surprise of everyone, he turned it down. He took a job at the State's Attorney's office instead, for less than half what we'd offered him. Now, looking back, I should have understood, because Blake had spent a lot of time talking with me about his future. And I was pretty sure Blake Canavan wanted to become a judge.

"Mike," he said now, patting my shoulder. "Gee whiz, how you been?"

"I'm doing pretty good, Blake. Good to see you."

"You're doing what, now?"

"I'm a private investigator. You still putting bad guys in jail?"

"Yeah, I'm down at 26th and California. Prosecuting murders, that's all I do now. Listen, Mike, come on over, I want you to meet my fiancé."

The woman smiled over from the other table—shoulder-length auburn hair, high cheekbones, elegant jaw line—I guessed her to be a lawyer. We went over and Blake introduced me. "This guy's my idol, Kris," he said. "A lawyer's lawyer. Mike taught me everything I know."

She extended a hand. I shook it.

"A used-to-be lawyer," I corrected. "But thank you."

"Well, used-to-be, whatever. In my book, you're still the best I've met."

Kris said, "Actually, Blake has told me a lot about you." That probably meant she knew all about my sordid past. But her smile seemed genuine.

"Sit down, join us," Blake said.

"Sorry, got an early one tomorrow." I said good night.

Driving north on the Kennedy, I thought about it, how I'd happened to run into Blake at a moment when my spirits were bumping against rock bottom. He'd lifted me up in a way he would never know. I'm not a religious person, but it does seem to make a good case for divine providence. Or at least a guardian angel hanging over my shoulder.

The following afternoon I sat at my office window staring at the row of newspaper vending machines across the street, trying to come up with a plan for what to do when I found Akibu—for I was going to find him. And here, remarkable in its brilliance, is the idea I came up with: *I'll cross that bridge when I come to it.*

My thoughts turned to Kim Price. She knew where Akibu was *and* she knew something terrible about him, and for the second time in twenty-four hours my gut squirmed with the thought that she was already dead. What had she been talking about that night? What could that something terrible be? What else *could* it be? Akibu had been hanging around the abandoned building at the time Reggie was kidnapped, and Akibu was desperately trying to keep from being found. If I could somehow get a sample of his DNA into police hands, maybe then I could persuade them to compare it to the semen found on Reggie's body. But how?

And who—or what—was Moody? It occurred to me that Marty might have some idea. I dialed the Deering District Police Station.

"It's Lieutenant Richter's day off," the desk sergeant told me.

I needed to settle some matters about my mother's funeral, and Marty lived in Mount Greenwood, not far from Kerrigan's. I picked up my car and drove out to the south side.

I headed south on the Dan Ryan with the windows open. Since the air conditioner of my aging Omni had breathed its last, I welcomed the fall weather, but on this day summer had made another counter-attack, overrunning Chicago with a moist, warm air mass from the Gulf. The temperature was hanging in the high seventies.

Mount Greenwood was on the city's southwest edge, its streets lined with neat green lawns and modest brick bungalows that were built during the housing boom when the GIs came home from World War II. You could say it was Chicago's version of Levittown, a little more upscale, maybe. But now, because the police were required to reside in the city, and because this was about as close to the border as you could get, it seemed as though a copper occupied every other house. I sometimes thought that if Marty stood on his front stoop and shouted loud enough, he could conduct roll call right there.

Sitting on the stoop is where I found him, as the sun was slipping down behind his house, a garden hose in his hand, wearing a Hawaiian shirt and shower shoes, his pink knees protruding from a pair of oversized khaki shorts. He twisted the nozzle to shut off the jet of water, but did not get up.

"Sun's below the yardarm," he said. "Want a drink?"

"Thought you'd never ask."

"Martini?"

"The perfect thing."

I followed him inside. Donna got up from the kitchen table and gave me a hug. "We don't see enough of you anymore," she said. "Can you stay for dinner, Mike?"

"Thanks, Donna. I can't."

"Yes, he is," Marty interrupted. Then to me, "You got some kind of pressing engagement?"

"Well, no," I said. We carried the drinks out to the yard, a modest square of lawn between the garage and the house edged with flowers, and sat at a round table with an umbrella at its center. I felt happy to be there as the martini's glow settled over me, though a vague sense of loss was

drifting up like smoke from somewhere inside. I was en-
vying Marty's contentment, his stable life with Donna, his
house, his connection to a neighborhood, his career—all the
things I craved.

I told Marty about Kim Price, her frightened call. When
I mentioned that she'd disappeared, he put his glass down.

"When you say *disappeared*, you don't mean, like, a
missing person?"

"Yeah. Well—"

"Mike, just because you can't find her doesn't make her
a missing person."

"True. But my gut tells me something really bad's going
on."

He cocked his head and flicked up an eyebrow, an ambiguous gesture that may have been a small concession. "I have
to say, it is odd that this Akibu guy is so dead set against you
finding him. But the woman was distraught when she called
you. Sounds like your basic domestic disturbance. In the
current climate, that's supposed to be a big deal; we handle
domestic disputes a lot different these days. But human nature hasn't changed any since you left the job. They're still
fighting one minute, fucking the next."

"But she mentioned he was involved with Moody. Do
you have any idea what the hell that could be?"

"Moody?" His eyes moved in an arc. "Doesn't mean
anything to me. You sure that's what she said, Moody?"

"She repeated it, a couple of times."

"I'll ask around, but it doesn't ring any bells." He
laughed. "Only thing I can think of is the Moody Bible Institute. Give me your glass." He took it, went into the
house, came back in four minutes with a refill. "You still
think you saw a hyena?" He was fighting back a smirk.

"Nope. I know I did."

"I guess I still don't get why you think that's important to your case," he said.

"Finding out what's behind that animal will help me find this guy."

"You're still assuming there's a connection."

"Yep."

"Okay, Mike. I don't mean to bust your balls, God knows you were the best investigator I ever knew. Donna says to come in and eat."

We lingered over dinner, my sense of contentment growing, this warm connectedness with Marty and Donna, and I realized how much that kind of thing had drifted out of my life.

"Did Marty tell you he's retiring next year?" Donna asked. This surprised me.

"Donna," Marty said, an admonition.

"What?"

"*Thinking about* retiring."

"Okay, thinking. The way you were talking this afternoon, you were thinking pretty hard," she said. Then to me, "We've looked at a few places in Florida."

"This is kind of sudden," I said, a vague foreboding rising in my gut. "You can actually do that?"

"City's talking about a buyout. Those developments down around Orlando give you an awful lot of bang for your buck, Mike. You know, with our boys both gone now, last winter was the first time in a long time I had to shovel snow. I've about had it with Chicago."

"Mike," Donna said, "have you spoken to Beth since your Mom's funeral?"

"Not really," I said.

She leveled her gaze at me. "You deserve someone like her, Mike. And she deserves you. But you know what? She's not going to be available forever."

"Donna," Marty said.

"It's okay," I said. "What makes you think she's available now?"

She paused a second, eyes still locked on mine. Then she said, "Take it from me, she's available. But maybe not next week, next month. You can't just expect—"

"Donna," Marty interrupted. "That's really none of your business."

"It's okay, Marty," I said.

Donna patted the back of my hand. "We worry about you. Don't let her slip away."

CHAPTER FOURTEEN

The following day, summer was once again in full retreat, and the maple trees along Peterson blazed like golden torches in the autumn sun. I parked the Omni near Magic Moments Beauty Salon and went in, a single dried leaf skittering ahead of me through the open door.

The owner came out of the back again to talk to me. She said that Kim hadn't shown up for work for several days, and no one had heard from her.

I drove back to her apartment building, and rang her bell. When she didn't answer, I rang the landlord's bell.

She came down to the glass door but didn't open it. "Have you seen Kim?" I asked.

"No, I haven't," she said, eyeing me suspiciously. "Is there some problem?"

"She hasn't been to work," I said.

"Well?" Her tone said she didn't see how that was my business. She did not seem concerned.

I gave her my card. "If you hear from Kim, will you ask her to call me?"

She studied the card with no expression, then lifted her eyes to mine. "You're a private detective?"

"Uh-huh."

"Didn't you say you were a friend of hers?"

"Right," I said. "I am." I started to leave, then said, "I'm both. Have you seen her since the last time I was here?"

"I really don't know," she said, pitching her eyes to the

bottom of the door. She pulled it shut.

I returned to the beauty parlor a few days later; this time the manager was standing at the cash register when I came in. Before I could say a word, she said in a tone that would freeze motor oil, "Kimberly Price no longer works here."

"Did she quit?"

"She is no longer employed at this beauty establishment; that is all I can tell you."

"Can I give you my card?" I handed one to her. "I really need to find her, it's important."

She read the card, gripping it in two hands as though it might escape, then looked at me. "I thought you said she's a friend of yours."

"She is," I said, with an attack of *déjà vu*. The corners of her lips lurched into a skeptical smile. She turned away wordlessly and disappeared into the back.

"Can I have one of those?" It was a beautician, a plump blonde wearing rhinestone-framed glasses, fortyish trying to look twenty-five. She was pulling a comb through a customer's wet hair. I'd noticed her the last time I was here, and thought then that I caught a spark of flirtation in her eyes.

I handed her my card. "Do you know where I might find Kim?"

Just then the manager came out from the back again, spotted us talking. Glaring, she started in my direction.

"Sorry," the beautician said, and turned quickly to the customer's hair.

With the manager bearing down on me malevolently, I left.

That evening after dinner, Beth called. "You'll never

guess who I had lunch with," she said.

I ruminated a full ten seconds. "Justin Ambertoe."

"Mike—have you been spying?"

"I'm a detective, remember?"

"Come on, how did you know?"

"I just guessed. You two seemed to have hit it off pretty well, at The Old Barn that night. You've got a lot in common, two artistic personalities. Sutler's Grove's a long way from boys' town, though."

"We met at Anne Sathers, and after lunch he showed me his studio. You've got to see his work, Mike. It's overwhelming. Awe-inspiring."

"I saw some of it. Contact sheets, anyway. But he gets some pretty important assignments. He does work for all the slick magazines."

"Yeah, but he was right when he said his best work is in black-and-white. You should see the subtle effects he creates in the dark room. He's got a darkroom set up in the basement of his apartment building, and he's also got a small gallery down there. It is positively staggering."

"Did you call to make me jealous?"

She laughed. "Of course. But really, you should make it a point to see his work; you'd love it." She paused. "I got to meet his friend, Richard. It's so sad, Mike; he looks like a perfect skeleton, he can't weigh fifty pounds, has IVs and constant oxygen. Justin says there's no way he'll have him dying in a hospital. You should see Justin with him, his devotion—it just breaks your heart."

I asked how her own business was going. "I'm afraid it's getting to be more work than fun, sometimes. Oh, which reminds me, I put that flyer in the mail to you, about the art fair. Did you get it?"

"No. When did you mail it?"

"Day before yesterday. Let me know, okay?"

I said goodbye and hung up, manic as usual after talking to her. I didn't know whether she'd take me back, even if I could convince her of my undying fidelity, but I believed she loved me. Had it not been for Justin Ambertoe, Beth would not be calling me. Justin didn't know it, but he'd brought a little joy back into my life, and at that moment I could have kissed him smack on the lips.

The evening news carried a story about the missing girl, Lawanda Henry. There was some footage of scuba divers emerging from the Washington Park lagoon, then cutting to sheriff's deputies on horseback in Dan Ryan Woods. "A mound thought to be a shallow grave turned out to be a compost heap," the reporter said. Then came an interview with the mother in her home, the camera drifting from her face to a photograph on the mantle, Lawanda in her first communion dress and veil, then to the mother again. She read a prepared statement, an appeal to whoever took her daughter to please return her safely. She managed to keep her voice even until the end, when she looked directly into the camera and ad-libbed. "Please, she's a good girl. She never did nothin' to hurt nobody." Her voice cracked, and she broke down.

The next story made me sit up.

"In other news tonight," the anchor said, "something is killing dogs in the Humboldt Park neighborhood. Earlier today, Lorenzo Townsend reported to police that his toy poodle had wandered off last evening. Apparently someone had forgotten to close the back gate. A search during the evening hours proved fruitless. Early this morning, how-ever, the poodle was found by a neighbor several blocks away, dead and partially eaten. Gary Weintraub has the story. Gary?"

The picture switched to Gary standing in a residential alley next to a garage door. "Jim, I'm standing in the exact spot where the poodle was found by a resident of the house to my right, who was able to identify the owner of the dog from the tags on its collar." The view panned downward, to a halo of bright light on blank concrete, and back. "Police are investigating. This is the second time in a week that a dog has been found dead this way."

"Gary, do the police have any theories?"

"I spoke to a patrol sergeant at the thirteenth district this afternoon, Jim. He said it's common for stray dogs to roam the neighborhood at night, sometimes in packs. This was a pretty small dog. They think that's what it was. Police do advise keeping pets inside."

"What can you tell us about the earlier incident?"

"The owner of the dog in that incident didn't actually report it until he'd learned that the poodle was found here. That one happened about two weeks ago. But the incidents were similar. His dog got out somehow, and he found it the following morning on the front parkway."

The picture returned to the studio, and the anchor said, "More news after this." I picked up the remote, snapped off the TV and called Marty Richter at home.

"I think I know why you're calling," he said. "Is it about the dead dogs?"

"Yeah. You know about it?"

"I signed the reports. Channel Seven had a camera crew in the station. For Christ's sake, I couldn't believe it. It's a non-story."

"Well, what do you think, then?"

"I think on a slow news day these guys know how to manufacture a story, especially with so many gullible people out there. Like a certain guy I know. Look, somebody's wimpy little poodle got torn up by a pack of dogs. I still can't believe they ran that story."

"I saw that fucking hyena, Marty."

"Yeah, I know. I thought of giving your phone number to Gary Weintraub, just to get the pain in the ass out of my station. You could've been on the evening news, Mike; you could've held up a Bible and told the world you see things. How's tomorrow night for dinner?"

We decided to meet at The Old Barn, and I hung up thinking that the stray dog theory was actually a plausible explanation. In the old days, when I'd worked the midnight watch in the inner city, packs of dogs commonly drifted up and down the alleys, moving from garbage can to garbage can. I used to wonder where they came from. Some even wore collars.

CHAPTER FIFTEEN

I opened the bedroom window wide and went to bed, the cool breeze toying with the curtains, and drifted off dreaming that I was still married to Beth, that I was still a lawyer. Life was sweet. Then came that foreboding lump in my stomach that foreshadowed disaster.

Then I was awake, sitting up, not sure why. The clock said 2:10. I listened a moment and then I heard it, something like the creak of a footstep on the back porch, no more than ten feet from the open window. In the darkness I swept my hand across the floor next to the bed, located my trousers, slipped them on. I found the Sig Sauer .380 on the night table, gripped the slide with the other hand and sat on the bed listening. There was no sound for half a minute. Then a definite shifting of weight on the porch floorboards. I pulled the slide back, chambering a round, the *che-chenk* louder than I expected. Whoever was out there bolted down the stairs.

I lunged for the light switch, stumbled into my loafers, ran to the back door, heard the intruder's footsteps hit the bottom of the stairs as I undid the lock, then from the porch I caught a glimpse of him tearing toward the back gate. I ran to the stairs, but something soft and wet and heavy smacked against my face. I stopped, looked back in confusion and saw Butler in the light from the kitchen, swinging from a wire wrapped around his neck, his coat soggy with blood, his belly sliced open, intestines dangling out like blue pasta.

Fire ignited my brain. I rushed down the stairs, across the yard, flung open the gate, and looked both ways down the alley, the surface glazed in dim orange light from the street lamp at the corner. Nothing moved; the alley was empty except for trashcans, and a van parked behind a garage to my left, a hundred feet away. I leaned a shoulder against the gatepost, holding the pistol downward in two hands, and yearned to kill the son of a bitch who did this.

He couldn't have gone far. I listened, a bus starting up on Armitage like a distant vacuum cleaner. I edged down the alley, hugging the garage door, then the neighbor's cyclone fence, keeping an eye on the van. Whoever it was could have crawled underneath.

About thirty feet from the van I squatted for a look, trying to remember if it had been parked there before, wishing I'd grabbed a flashlight. I could see, against the backdrop of the lit surfaces at the end of the alley, that nothing was under it. There was no sound, no movement, only the faint smell of garbage from the three containers to my left.

Those containers—it struck me that someone could be crouching behind them.

And in the same instant, a man leapt up from behind them and bolted toward the van, almost close enough to touch, and I lunged for him, swung an arm around his neck, shoved the pistol into my waistband as we both stumbled to the concrete. He regained his feet, spun and, as I was getting up, he caught me with a wild swing to the jaw, but the punch was weak, and I gained my feet and drove into him with both forearms, shoving him backward against a fence; then, rage boiling up in me, I went to work on him, a series of left jabs to his face. I felt his nose break, then smashed a roundhouse right into the side of his head and he slid to the ground. I grabbed a fistful of his shirt, but he scrambled and pulled free and, still sitting, scooted a few feet to the middle of the alley; but before he could get up, I kicked him hard in the chest. He folded himself into a fetal ball, then. I stood over him, raised a foot to stomp his head but he rolled against my legs. I fell over him.

I was sprawling there in the middle of the alley when the van's lights came on. The engine cranked and roared, dropped into gear and it came barreling toward me. I rolled against the other guy, felt the soft rush of air as the tire passed my face. It screeched to a stop next to the two of us; the passenger door swung open and the guy scrambled over me, trying to climb in. I grabbed a leg but he kicked me away, and then he was inside and the door slammed shut and the van squealed off.

I got to my feet, drew the Sig Sauer, and emptied seven shots into the back of the van, the glass in the back doors shattering as it accelerated to the end of the alley. It turned the corner and was gone.

I considered running to my car, which was parked out in front. But the keys were up in the apartment. I stood a moment, searing into my memory the image of that van. Blue, some damage to the right rear quarter panel, a tail light missing on that side. It was too dark to get the license number, but now at least it had some unique identifying characteristics, a few .380 holes in the back.

I was wishing I'd gotten a better look at the guy. He was white, late twenties, skinny, long dark hair. That was all that registered.

Then the enormity of what I'd just done began settling over me like the smell of garbage. I'd shot at a moving vehicle, could have killed someone, and had no legal justification for the use of deadly force. I went back upstairs quickly, past poor Butler hanging there, locked the back door, turned off all the lights and went to bed.

But as I lay there, the walls started pulsing with red and blue lights as one squad car, then another, came speeding down the alley. I realized I owed it to Fred Habranek to report what happened to Butler to the police. I turned on the lights, dialed 911, told the dispatcher that I'd heard gunshots in the alley.

"It's already been reported," she said. "The police are on the way."

"But wait." I told her about Butler hanging out there. She confirmed my name and address, said they'd be there shortly. "They're here now," I said. "Tell them I'll be on the back porch, to come up the back way." I didn't want them coming to the front door, parading through the apartment to the back porch. Not all of my guns were registered, and I had no idea what they might claim they saw in plain view. Besides, someone might stretch that into a consent to search my place.

I flicked the porch light on for the first time that evening, and got a good look at poor Butler. The side of his head was bashed in, his fur matted with blood. I left him for the police to examine.

The two officers who came up the back stairs wouldn't let me cut him down, and we stood there in the glare of the single bulb, Butler swinging between us, the younger of the two asking questions, scribbling out a case report on a clipboard. The older one did not seem to believe me. *I* would not have believed me.

"Let me see if I've got it straight," he said. "The gunshots woke you up?"

I nodded.

"You went out on your back porch and found the cat. And you heard a van drive off. Did it drive off before or after you went out on the porch?"

"Before."

"Then how did you know it was a van?"

I looked down the row of back yards to the end of the block. You could see the side street from here. "I saw it after it turned out of the alley and headed north," I said, pointing.

"It headed north?"

I nodded again.

"How many people were in the van?"

Tricky. "I have no idea."

"And you have no idea who they were?"

"None."

"And of course you have no idea why they would have killed your cat and hung it outside your door?"

I lifted my shoulders, turned my palms up. "It's my landlord's cat."

"Is your landlord home?"

"He's out of town. Actually, I was looking after the cat." His eyes held mine and would not let go. I refused to blink.

Finally he said, "Okay, if they come back, call us. And don't shoot at anyone, okay?"

"Can I take the cat down, now?"

He thought a moment. "No, we'll have the evidence technician get some pictures."

I went back to bed but couldn't sleep. The police were out there for a long time, radios hissing and squawking, and I got up, looked out the window. Then I jumped, startled by a face a foot away from mine. "Sorry," the uniformed officer said as I opened the door. "I just need to take some pictures." I stood on the porch as he snapped pictures of Butler from several angles. "This is a real shame," he said. "Your cat?"

"He belonged to my landlord."

The officer shook his head, stuffing his camera into a bag; then he pulled out a flashlight and held it low, scanning the beam across the floor. "We picked up a few .380 casings from the alley. You own any guns?"

"No."

"Right," he said, in a tone that seemed to question my veracity, then picked up his bag and left.

I locked my back door once again, gunshots still echoing in my head. I couldn't think of going to sleep. I sat in my living room chair and stared at the black TV screen, the gunshots mingling with others from another time.

I was a policeman back then, involved in an affair with a woman who lived on my beat. Her husband, a guy who'd called me his friend, worked nights.

One evening when I was off-duty, I made an excuse to Beth to get out of the house. I drove to their house in Hyde Park, parked behind twin condominium buildings across the street. It was a regular routine, parking there, threading my way between the condo buildings, then crossing the street and sneaking around to her back door.

But this time was different. As I came around a corner into the courtyard between the buildings, a man in a ski mask stepped from the shadows with a gun in his hand. Without a word, he started blazing away at me. A bullet grazed my abdomen and another shattered my ankle, and as I fell I drew my service revolver, fired five shots in quick succession.

I killed the guy right there. I crawled to him on my belly, pulled off the ski mask. It was the woman's husband. He'd been a really sweet guy. He'd trusted me—at least at first.

When the police came, they found me lying next to him, weeping like a child. They thought it was from the pain.

Well, it was. I've always liked to think that, had I known, I would have stood there and taken it like a man.

I did nearly lose my foot, and now I try not to limp when I walk. It was the end of my police career. But a brand new law career was waiting for me, only to be destroyed by my twin passion.

CHAPTER SIXTEEN

I met Marty at The Old Barn the following evening and brought him up to date on the investigation. I told him about the incident with Butler, about the blue van. He was unusually quiet during dinner; then, as we sipped cognac afterwards, he cleared his throat.

"Mike, I want to help you in any way I can. Help *you,* I mean, not that fudge-packer client of yours. He killed the kid. I know he did."

"If you knew him, you wouldn't say that. I know he didn't do it."

"Okay, let's get to the main point here," he said. "I can't believe you shot at the van, for Christ's sake."

"I know," I said.

"You know? What the hell were you thinking, 'you know.' Even when you were a copper, you never pulled any crap like that."

"I was really, really, really pissed," I said.

"Now there's a defense, buddy. 'Sorry, Your Honor, I just get really pissed off sometimes.' That might actually get your charge lowered to manslaughter. Good behavior, you're out in twenty years." He took a sip of brandy, then two-fingered a cigarette from his shirt pocket, lit it, snapped the Zippo shut. "You know, somebody could still turn up dead from a .380 slug. And you know as well as I do, if that happens, they'll come looking for your gun."

"I've thought about that."

"No matter which way you cut it, you couldn't justify

deadly force." He turned his face to blow away a cloud of smoke, then added, "Even if you were the police, which, please remember, you are not."

He didn't have to remind me, but I let it go. "He did try to run me over." I was sorry I said it; it was lame.

"You know, I'm not even going to respond to that. You're as familiar with the law as I am."

"Then let's change the subject. Where do I go from here?"

He shook his head. "Sorry, I can't help you there."

I didn't say anything. His eyes were cast down, his hand resting on the brandy snifter. He started making slow circles with it on the tablecloth. "Look, Mike. This whole thing's a little preposterous. Does it occur to you that it's just too co-incidental? You think you saw a hyena in the park. There's an African guy who, it so happens, lived on the same block where the kid was grabbed. So now this hyena—which, by the way, no one but you ever saw—this hyena is connected somehow to your murder investigation. Do you think . . ."

I interrupted. "The guy deals in African animal skins."

His eyebrows lifted in mock surprise. "Now there's a clue. So tell me, expert-on-African-wildlife, how much is a hyena skin worth?"

I shrugged, moving my eyes off his, and sipped my drink. He was going a little overboard, probably the residue of his agitation with my shooting at the van.

"There's leopard skin coats and zebra skin rugs. You ever see a hyena skin? I mean, without the hyena in it? I'll tell you, buddy, I've seen coats made of . . ."

"All right, Jesus, you made your point. But let me tell you something, I . . ."

He raised both palms. "Do you think that maybe the power of suggestion is working overtime on your brain here? Look, I understand you don't have much to go on. But that doesn't mean you just grab anything to fill in the blanks." He sat back, drained the last of his cognac, signaled the waitress to bring another.

Then he leaned on his arms.

"Sorry, Mike," he said in a softer tone, "I think I interrupted you. What were you going to say?"

"I think you're forgetting that's just the way it is, sometimes. Marty. Let me try playing your little trivia game. Here's a name from the distant past: Joshua Hill."

He didn't miss a beat. "Yeah, we busted him for a double bubble." What we called a double homicide.

"You remember how we happened to pick him up? You had a *dream*, for Christ sake."

Joshua Hill had fled the city, and though we were pretty sure he was somewhere back in rural Mississippi where he came from, he left no trail. The investigative file listed him as a known-but-flown.

Then one summer morning after roll call three years later, Marty told me he'd had a dream the night before, said he saw Joshua Hill sleeping in his old room on Lake Park, where he'd been staying with his auntie. We went straight from the station to the flat in Kenwood, and we found Joshua in his bed, sound asleep. He surrendered without an argument.

"So? What's that got to do with coincidence?"

"Wasn't the dream a coincidence?"

"It's different."

"How?"

"Don't ask me to explain how that works 'cause I don't know, it's just different. You're not talking about a dream, here. You're talking about a fucking hyena."

★ ★ ★ ★ ★

Driving home that night, I struggled with what to do next. Now more than ever I wanted to find this son-of-a-bitch Akibu; it had gotten real personal. I knew in my gut he was connected to both the murder of Reggie Brockton and the disappearance of Lawanda Henry. Why else would he be taking me on? But without Kim Price, I had no idea how to find him. And I still had to connect him to the kidnapping of those two kids.

I lay awake most of the night, then overslept the following morning. At the kitchen table I only had time for a quick perusal of the paper, and I almost missed it. As I stood, taking a last sip of coffee, it caught my eye, a short article in The World section: "More Than Two Hundred Suspected Witches Killed."

I read it standing up. Natives in northeastern Congo were lynching suspected witches by the score, blaming them for outbreaks of disease. Troops from Uganda had to come in to bring the situation under control. "Sometimes *Sangomas,* the traditional healers of the region, are accused of crossing over into witchcraft," the article said.

Then something really grabbed my attention: "*Sangomas* use the organs of animals such as jackals and hyenas, in their ministrations."

Hyena organs. And Akibu was in the business of importing African artifacts. I sat down, read it again, my interest in those two guys from Texas suddenly renewed. It was still a stretch, but more than ever, I was convinced David Akibu was somehow connected to that hyena, and I wanted to know what they knew. There was no reason to believe they'd tell me anymore than they had that morning at the motel. But it couldn't hurt.

I still had Elmer's card with his phone number, but of the two of them, he seemed the more hostile. I could call the ranch, try to contact Nate that way. But even if I reached him, what could I say over the phone?

My chances of getting anywhere with the two cowboys were far greater if I could talk to them face to face. I called Julia Ambertoe in Houston.

"I'm not sure I understand," she said after I explained. "You want to fly to Texas?"

"Actually, yes."

"Then you should do it. I don't see the problem."

"In that case, is first class okay?"

"Is this more of your humor, Mr. Duncavan?"

That evening I microwaved a couple of Hungry Man dinners and, as I ate them with a cold bottle of Corona while watching the evening news, someone knocked on my door. It was Fred Habranek, home from his trip, grinning at me.

"So," he said. "How're Butler and Stapler getting along?"

CHAPTER SEVENTEEN

When I asked Fred to sit down, apprehension darkened his face like a cloud shadow. But he took the news stoically. He asked if I knew who did it. I said no, which was true. There was no point in explaining all about David Akibu. But as he sat there saying nothing, leaning on his knees and studying the carpet, I knew I couldn't leave it at that.

"Fred, I think it could have something to do with a case I'm working on. I think they're trying to get to me."

He just got to his feet without saying anything and went to the door. Then he said, "Well, if you find the fuckers, just let me have first crack at them, will you?"

I left for Texas the following day. I didn't have the heart to ask Fred to look after Stapler, so I put him in a kennel. I got a flight from O'Hare to Houston, took a connecting flight to El Paso, and rented a car. It was midafternoon when I pulled into the long gravel driveway of the Mesquite Bend Ranch, an eclectic collection of buildings that traced the transition from working cattle ranch to shooting lodge for the affluent.

I went into the main lodge, stood at a desk at the edge of a great room with a fireplace you could play a poker game in. Animal heads, a whole herd of them, lined the walls— gemsbok, blackbuck, aiudad, Barbary sheep. Except for the silent zoo, the place was empty. I called through the door behind the desk. "Hello?"

A woman about forty came out, hair like a red flame, a

little heavy in the hips, but a smile so friendly I nearly asked her to marry me.

"Can I hep yew?"

"I'm looking for an old friend, I think he works here. Nate Wilcox?"

Her smile melted down to a look of sympathy. "Oh, I'm sorry, he doesn't work here no more."

"Do you know how I might reach him?"

"I sure don't," she said.

"How about Elmer Bumpp?"

Her eyes brightened a little. "Well, Elmer doesn't work here no more, neither. But he's got a place over to Meltrey? He's a dog trainer, you know, pretty highly thought of hereabouts. He's had some champions."

She gave me directions to Meltrey, just down the road a hundred miles.

It was almost dark when I came to his place ten miles off the main highway down a washboard road, a double-wide, green aluminum siding with garage and kennels to match. I pulled into the yard, my car caked with yellow dust, and before I shut off the engine a blue-tick hound behind a chain link fence broke into a wail, then what sounded like a stadium full of dogs joined in. As I was getting out of the car, Elmer Bumpp came onto the porch in his undershirt.

He nodded in greeting as I came up the flagstone walk, his smile cordial until he recognized me. "Christ on a crutch," he said. "What the hell do you want?"

"Can we sort of start over again?" I extended a hand. "I just need to talk to you." He looked at my hand as if I'd just finished picking up dog droppings, but then he took it, his fingers like chipped broomsticks.

"We won't be able to hear ourselves think out here. Come on inside." He led me into the living room, Vanna White turning letters on the television screen, waved me to the couch and snapped the TV off. "Guess you know, I don't work for the ranch no more," he said, settling into an easy chair.

"Yeah. And you know I'm not with the police. I've been working on the murder of a little kid. Now another little kid is missing from the same neighborhood. Maybe it's not too late to save her."

"If you're not working for the police, who are you working for?"

"A man who's been wrongly accused."

He stared. "What's any of this got to do with me?"

"Probably nothing, but I think there could be a connection with a hyena, somehow."

He put his hands on his knees and leaned forward, gave me a long, curious look without saying anything. "What kind of connection would that be?"

"Just a hunch. I guarantee I won't get you into any trouble."

"I'd just like to know. What kind of connection?"

"I think whoever you dealt with had something to do with the murder, though I'll admit it's pretty weak. Then again, it usually is at the start."

He studied my face for several seconds, and said, "Okay, I'll tell you what I know, but I don't see what it could have to do with missing kids."

This is what he told me. He and Nate had been ranch hands at Mesquite Bend, which still ran some cattle, though the big money seemed to be in exotic game ranching. Neither he nor Nate had anything to do with that part of the operation, but one day the owner approached the two of them with a proposition: drive a pickup truck to Chicago and deliver a pair of hyenas.

"It was all very hush-hush," he said. "I figured the animals were illegal as hell."

"Did he tell you that?"

"Not in so many words, but I knew when they arrived at the ranch, they didn't come through regular channels. It was common knowledge around the place." He laughed, scratched the back of his neck. "I think he asked me because I'm an experienced dog handler, if you can imagine that. But the pay was damn good—cash, too. He asked me if I had a couple big dog kennels, and I said, 'Sure.'

"Right there turned out to be a problem. Plain stupidity, I guess, but I never thought nothing of it 'til we tried to load the hyenas from the enclosure, and I realized it was the wrong kind of a cage for an animal like that. See, your regular kennel has a door that swings open, just like any door. What we should've had was one to where you could put it right up against the enclosure and drive the animal in, a door that slides up and down. Your regular dog kennel leaves a gap. We got them loaded, all right, but we had one hell of a time of it, I can tell you that.

"I worried all the way to Chicago about how we was gonna get them unloaded. We met the buyer in the park that night, and you can guess what happened. Surer'n shit, when we were unloading them, the female got out, took off across the park. Hell, looking back on it, I should've just given him the animals in the kennels and let him keep them, but they was my property and I wanted them back. Plain stupid.

"Well, the guy refused to pay us, said he ordered a breeding pair. One was no good to him, he said."

"He intends to breed hyenas?"

Elmer shrugged. "He said, 'breeding pair,' and that's all I know."

"So, you didn't take the other one back with you?"

"And try to load the sonofabitch again, drive it all the way back to Texas? No fucking way, Jose."

"Do you know the buyer's name?"

He smiled at me like I was a kid asking him the meaning of a dirty word. "There was no names. All we were supposed to do was meet this guy in a blue van in the park, transfer the animals and pick up an envelope with four thousand dollars.

"When we got back home, the boss fired us on the spot. Balls, no surprise there. I really didn't give a shit, anyway; that whole business made me feel like some kind of a low-life. That and runnin' around the park like a couple of retards trying to get the animal back. Served us right, I guess. We're pretty honest people; I never got mixed up in anything illegal in my entire life. Felt like a fucking drug dealer or something." He came forward in his chair. "If you're wondering why I'm telling you this, that's the reason. I want to do the right thing."

"What did the buyer look like?"

"They was two of 'em. Guy in charge was black, maybe thirty-five, talked with some kind of accent, I couldn't hardly understand him. The other guy was white, twenty-five to thirty maybe, real skinny, looked like a damn hippie, real long hair, kept brushing out of his eyes. And a tattoo right here." He tapped the inside of his left forearm. "A heart with a dagger through it."

"What about the black guy? Anything else you can tell me about the way he looked?"

"Naw, he was average height, average build. Only thing that'd stand out would be his accent."

"Do you know anything about him at all? I mean, from what your boss told you?"

"Just that he's in the import business, that's what I was told. He imports carvings and shit from Africa."

"You said they were driving a van?"

"Yeah, it was a full-sized van, Dodge Ram I think, dark blue, one tail light busted out. Looked like it had been rear-ended on the one side. Right rear quarter panel was pushed in a little. It gave them some trouble getting the damn door shut."

It was dark when I left, insects flickering around the yellow light as we stood on the porch, a faint fragrance of sage in the air.

"I'd like to help in any way I can," Elmer said. "You maybe wanta think about calling me first, though, stedda dropping by. It's kind of a long trip."

On the flight back I took a window seat and passed on the meal. Instead, the flight attendant poured two of those miniature bottles of Stolichnaya over ice and set a third un-opened one on the tray with two bags of peanuts. Growing mellow, I ruminated, one peanut at a time, on the nature of criminal investigation, the role of intuition, the playing of hunches. And coincidence. Marty Richter thought I was chasing shadows. But whatever connection Akibu had with those missing kids, there was no longer any doubt that he was responsible for the hyena in Humboldt Park.

I knew David Akibu murdered Reggie Brockton. He was hanging around that building when Reggie disappeared, and now he was desperately trying to shake me off his track. I had no doubt his fingerprints were on Reggie's scooter, along with Justin's. The same David Akibu tried to buy a pair of breeding hyenas—there was a connection there somewhere.

Finding him wasn't going to be easy. He was in the import business; he drove a blue Dodge van with a busted tail light. And a few bullet holes. That was about it.

Then I remembered something. The day I'd called the Brookfield Zoo, the woman told me someone else called the same day, wanting to sell hyenas. Or did she say hyena, singular? If Akibu needed a breeding pair, one would be no good to him—maybe he was trying to sell it.

The lady said she fielded those calls for the director, which meant she would have taken down a phone number. Maybe she still had it, and maybe she'd give it to me. Another long shot, but nearly every shot I took these days had to be a three-pointer.

CHAPTER EIGHTEEN

It was two a.m. when I got home from the airport, so I slept late the following morning, then drove through a steady drizzle to Des Plaines to spring Stapler from the kennel, and dropped him at home.

Traffic on the inbound Kennedy oozed through the rain, and I didn't get to the office until after two o'clock. Exposed to full daylight and lacking the soft focus vodka provided, my idea of calling the zoo seemed pretty lame. Even if they still had the number, why would they give it to me? I could say I was from another zoo, but I didn't talk zoo talk—they'd catch on to that right away.

But a bad idea is better than no idea at all, and I came up with a lame plan to match. I called Brookfield Zoo, asked for the librarian, and said, "This is Melvin Ross. I work at the small mammal house at Lincoln Park Zoo—I'm not part of the administration or anything, but I have this kind of crazy request."

She laughed. "Well, we get a lot of those. How can I help you?"

"I heard that someone called our zoo a couple of weeks ago wanting to sell a hyena. I mean, he didn't call the small animal house, he called the zoo administration office, but our administration wasn't interested. Anyway, I told my cousin about it—he works at the Memphis Zoo—and he says they're looking for hyenas. I asked at the main office, but now no one here can find the guy's number. I thought he might have called you folks, and maybe—I know this is kind of farfetched, but maybe he called you and you had the guy's number. That is, if you folks weren't interested in buying it yourselves."

"You know, we did get a call like that. I would have referred it to the director. Would you like to speak to him?"

"No, no, I'm just wondering if you still might have that number."

"Well, like I say, I would have given the message to the director."

"Could you connect me with him, then?" I had nothing to lose. Luckily, I got his voice mail. I punched "0" and asked to be transferred back to the librarian.

"I'm afraid he's out," I said. "Is there any chance you'd still have that number?"

An edge of irritation came into her voice. "Like I told you before, I would have given it to him." Then her voice softened. "Wait. I might have a carbon copy of the message slip. Just a minute, can you hang on?"

Could I hang on? *By my fingernails, lady.* I waited, afraid to breathe.

"Here it is," she said. "His name is David Akibu: 773-555-3986."

I wanted to climb through the wires and kiss her on both cheeks, on her arms, her neck. I got up and danced around my desk until an icy poker stabbed my ankle and I sat down and dialed the cross directory service. The phone was listed to Thaddeus Temple, with an Edgebrook address. Every once in a while, things do fall into place. I drove directly to Edgebrook.

It was a single family Tudor on a pleasant, shaded street. A middle-aged, heavyset man in suspenders, white shirt open at the neck, opened the door.

"Pardon me, I'm looking for Mr. David Akibu," I said.

He looked at me blankly, waiting for me to go on. I didn't.

"Who?" he asked from behind the screen.

I repeated the name.

"I don't know anyone by that name." He gave me a chilly smile. "Sorry." He started to close the door when a woman inside said, "Ted! You do too! That's Clyde's friend from Africa."

The woman appeared in the doorway in a blue warm-up suit, her husband disappearing into the house without saying more. She was middle-aged, chubby, blonde hair in curlers. "Can I help you?"

"I'm hoping you can. Mr. Akibu has a very sick relative in Africa. I need to find him."

"Oh, my. And you're with who, the police?"

"No, ma'am. American Red Cross." I wished I was a quicker thinker, but she bought it.

"Oh. Well, David Akibu is a friend of our son's. I don't know where he is."

"Your son?"

"No, sorry, I mean I don't know where David is. Our son is on vacation in San Francisco; he's coming home next week. David stayed with us for a few days. Such a nice, polite man, I wish I could help." She turned into the house. "Ted," she called. "Ted, could you come here?" Ted returned.

"The man needs to find David, it's urgent. Someone is sick in his family. Can you think how we might find him?"

The man eyed me. "I don't know nothing about him. Clyde brought him home." Disapproval etched his face. "The guy stayed in the basement a few days, that's all I know."

"Can I can get in touch with your son?" I asked. "It's Clyde?"

"Yes, Clyde, but I don't know where he's staying. He'll be home next week," she repeated, trying to be encouraging.

I took out one of my cards, then remembered I was working for the Red Cross, but it was too late. "Here's my card," I said. She pushed the screen door open, took it. "I do *pro bono* work for the Red Cross; they don't have full-time investigators. If you hear from your son, please have him call me."

She bought it. She looked at it and smiled, and I left, wishing I could have talked to the father alone. There was something about his displeasure that seemed worth exploring.

The thought of it rested on my mind like a paperweight as I headed back to the Loop on the Kennedy, and finally I picked up my cell phone and dialed the Temple residence. He answered.

"Mr. Temple, sorry to bother you again. I got the feeling when we talked that maybe you didn't completely approve of David Akibu."

"And I get the feeling you're not with the Red Cross."

I ignored it. "Anything I can learn about him might help. Was there something you didn't like about David Akibu?"

"There's something I don't like about my son's lifestyle, but I don't see how that's any of your business."

"Can you just tell me what you mean by his lifestyle?"

"And there's something I don't like about you," he said, and the next thing I heard was a dial tone.

At the office I called Stan Janda to give him an update. When he answered the phone, I could tell by the lead weight in his voice that there was something wrong. It didn't take him long to tell me what.

"The cops picked up Justin early this morning," he said. "They've charged him with murder. The DNA test results came back, and the semen on the boy's body matches Justin's."

It took me a few seconds to be sure I understood. "Wait, you mean . . . ?"

"I mean it's Justin Ambertoe's DNA."

It hit me like a sucker punch. I didn't say anything.

"His bond hearing's tomorrow morning," Stan said.

"So, what happens now?"

"I don't know, Mike. The case against him couldn't be worse. The only thing I can hope for now is to keep him from the death penalty, but I have a feeling the State won't want to deal at this point. The detectives let Justin call me from the station, so I talked to him this morning." He paused. "He had an unusual request. He asked me to call your ex-wife."

"Did you call her?"

"Yeah, but maybe you want to give her a call, too."

"Anything else you want me to do?"

"Keep working. That's what his mother says. I just got off the phone with her. She wants to get an independent DNA test. You find anything good in Texas?"

"Nothing worth talking about," I said. "Stan, I don't know much about DNA testing, but I've never heard of a case where the results were wrong."

"Neither have I, Mike." He hung up without saying goodbye.

I turned my chair to the window, a river of rain-glazed umbrellas floating down Washington Street, and grappled with the new information, tried to make sense of it. All I could think was that Ambertoe really did murder that kid, and I was trying to help him. But then I saw Justin in my mind's eye. He just wasn't capable of it—he couldn't have done it.

Or could he?

I called Beth.

"He couldn't have done it, Mike," she said, "I know he couldn't. I just don't understand this. What do you think is going on?"

"Beth . . . he could have." I heard the rain pattering against my window. A truck started up from the light.

"You can't possibly believe that," she said, an icicle hanging from her words.

"Sometimes it goes like that," I said. "I can't close off possibilities."

"Oh, how profound. Droppings of wisdom from Mike Duncavan."

This was turning ugly. "I've got to go, Beth."

"You're supposed to be working for him. Who's paying you? Don't you think you owe it to him to have a little faith, for God's sake?"

"I've got to go, Beth."

"All right." Then calmer, "If you need to get hold of me, I'll be staying at Justin's apartment."

"You *what?*"

"I need to make some arrangements for Richard."

"Beth, you hardly know these people."

"Better than you do, I'd say."

"Let the police worry about Richard. They're not going to abandon him there."

"No, they won't abandon him; they've already called in some social service agency. They want to put him in a nursing home. That wasn't Justin's plan. Or Richard's. He doesn't have long, Mike. But I suppose you don't see that as your problem."

"I'm sure they have their own friends."

"I'm sure they do. I'm going to see how many I can contact, so we can work something out."

I said goodbye. Justin and Richard. Richard and Justin. Where did this come from?

Before going to bed that evening I had a couple of drinks, which is probably what did it. Mellowed out on Stoli, I got to thinking about what Beth said, about owing Justin loyalty. It was tough to accept that he could be a child murderer. Then again, it was tough to accept that he wasn't. I thought again of those photographs he took, the scooter in that abandoned apartment, the emotion of those images, their power. And then I thought of David Akibu, and of Kim Price's words: *He's evil.*

And where was Kim Price now?

I had to give Justin the benefit of the doubt, even though I was having trouble finding some doubt. It was simply a matter of resolving it and moving on. Besides, I needed the money.

I didn't go to bed then. I poured one more Stoli over the rocks and located the newspaper article about the lynching of witches in the Congo, the one that had mentioned hyena organs and the practice of *muti*. I went to the computer and got on the Net, plugged in the word *"muti."* I got no hits.

Then I plugged in "traditional healing," and it was as if I'd up-ended a cornucopia of information. I labored through a wealth of articles on the subject, and soon I was beginning to find references to *muti*. Apparently there are *muti* markets throughout southern Africa, where you can buy hyena bones, dried monkey heads, baboon fingers, powdered animal organs, all sold for their magical, medicinal powers.

But I discovered a much darker side. The most powerful *muti* of all was human—human organs removed from live victims, preferably children: hearts, kidneys, livers. According to one article, "The requisite body parts cannot come from naturally deceased bodies, like transplant organs. To be effective, they must be taken from a person who is alive at the time, and who ceases, in the process, to continue living. Ideally, death should not have occurred long before the *muti* is put to use."

I found an article from the *Johannesburg Chronicle*:

> *Three hundred sixty-six children have gone missing in the four northern provinces in three years—one child every three days.*
>
> *According to Detective Dieter Braacht of the occult crime section of the Johannesburg police, only about sixty of the three hundred muti murders he's investigated ever got to court. Of those, there were very few convictions. "It is very, very difficult to find witnesses. You go to the villages; the people will not speak of this. They are terrified. They know that when they come out of the courtroom, they will die."*

The *Cape Town Independent* carried this story: *Muti Killing: Boy of Ten Goes to Court.*

> *The ten-year-old boy, accused of taking part in the gruesome muti murder of a toddler, has appeared in the Pietermaritzburg magistrate's court, along with a man of thirty-nine.*
>
> *The boy and Samson Mholophe were appearing the second time after their arrest three weeks ago for the apparent muti killing of a three-year-old girl, Thabile*

Mhlanzi. Her body was mutilated while she was still alive; her tongue, ears, and genital areas were cut off. She was found, still breathing, by neighbors. The boy is alleged to have been paid R25 for fetching the child.

My head resonated with the terrified voice of Kim Price: *He is evil—an evil, evil man. He's involved with Moody.* And suddenly, sweat prickling the top of my spine, I knew she wasn't talking about somebody named Moody. She was telling me that Akibu practiced *muti*—the human variety.

CHAPTER NINETEEN

A sunny fall day was in full bloom next morning, the traffic heading into the Loop moving reasonably well for that hour, until I crossed Canal Street. There it stopped, horns blaring as I inched along in the curb lane, and I could see traffic ahead jockeying around a green mini-van with its flashers on.

A plaza at that point stretches between the old *Daily News* building and a low wall overlooking the river, and a market was being set up there, an assemblage of white tents luffing in the wind. Two black women were shuttling arm-loads of clothing from the van. When I pulled directly behind it, I could see they were frazzled, and I even considered offering them a hand. Then the guy behind me leaned on his horn.

I wanted to walk back and have a little heart to heart, but I didn't. I maneuvered around the van, the very model of self-restraint. Not long ago, I would have walked back, plucked the horn-blower from his vehicle and performed some kind of adjustment upon his person.

But, after I left my car at the garage, I did walk back to the market. There were about twenty vendors, all of them ethnic—Guatemalan woolens, Indian carpets, African carvings. I strolled over to where a man was setting out rows of African masks on a table, and looked over a pair of tall, carved statues standing on the ground. One was a man with a stone axe over his shoulder, the other a woman carrying a large bowl. The wood was dark, the figures decorated in intricate beadwork.

"They are going to visit the king," the man said, smiling. His accent was so thick I could barely understand him. "She is carrying (something) to the king. The man is protecting her."

"Ah," I said. "A gift for the king?"

"No, no, no," he said. He explained again. I did not understand a word.

"Interesting," I said. "Where do they come from?"

"This is Yoruba, from Nigeria." He passed a hand over the masks. "Some are from Ghana, some from Uganda."

"Do you import them directly?"

"Some I do. I get them different ways."

"Do you happen to know an importer by the name of David Akibu? He's an old friend of mine. I'm afraid I've lost touch with him."

"Akibu?" He frowned, thinking. "No, I do not know him."

"Well, I hope this isn't an imposition," I said, taking out a card. I wrote "David Akibu" on the back, handed it to him. "David's moved," I said, "and I don't know how to go about contacting him. Maybe if you run across him, you could do me a great favor and call me?"

While he studied the card, I walked over, picked up a mask.

"How much is this one?" I asked.

After I paid him for the mask, he looked again at the back of the card, then raised it above his head. "So, this Mr. Akibu, he owes you money?" He was grinning.

"He's just an old friend," I said, in a way that let him know he might have guessed right. "I'd make it worth your while, if you could help me."

"Sure, I'll keep this. Thank you, Mister . . ." he flipped the card over. "Duncavan."

I stopped at the booth where the ladies were selling dresses. They seemed amused by my interest. "You have a girlfriend?" one asked, her accent clipped, elegant.

"I'm sorry to say that I do," I said.

"I'm sorry, too," she laughed, her pretty eyes toying with me. "Which one do you like?"

I bought a dress, then learned that neither of these women knew David Akibu. I left my card with them.

After I traversed the line of booths and my arms were full, I learned that none of the other African exhibitors knew Akibu, either.

At the office, I propped the wooden mask on the credenza next to Beth's picture and dialed Stan Janda. Then I hung up, not sure how to put what I wanted to tell him about *muti*. That whole business had a kind of fairy tale quality, yet we were fighting the most solid evidence the world of science had to offer. But when I considered the mutilated body of Reggie Brockton, his heart, liver, and kidneys taken, there seemed only one explanation for it. David Akibu, importer of hyenas, practitioner of *muti*. I dialed again.

After I explained, he didn't say anything for several seconds. Then he said, "I'm with you, of course, Mike. It's all we've got. But I'm not sure where you're going from here. I don't think the police will help us. They've got Ambertoe cinched up, case cleared. Face it. If you were them, what would you do?"

"Do you know who the prosecutor is?"

"Yeah, a guy says he knows you. Blake Canavan?"

Here might be a small break, I thought.

I said goodbye, called Blake at his office at Criminal Court on 26th Street. He seemed happy to hear from me, proving once again that life's troubles reveal your true friends.

"I need to tell you up front, Mike, I don't see what we can do for you guys on this one."

"I'm not the lawyer, that's up to Janda. If I get caught practicing law, they'll run me out of town. But it'd be nice if we could avoid a lot of formality in getting the discoverable stuff."

"Well, we've got no secrets, it's a pretty simple case. You know we got a DNA match, right?"

"Right."

"We'll turn everything over at the arraignment."

The arraignment was a week later. There was no need for me to be there, but I decided to go anyway, and not bill for the time. When I arrived, court was already in session, and I took a seat in the back row. Stan was sitting in the front row, Blake Canavan standing at the bench.

When the bailiff called "People v. Ambertoe," Justin was shuffled through a back door by a deputy sheriff, his hands joined behind him, his eyes like a caged animal's. He stood before the bench with his head bowed. But when he was asked how he pleaded, his tone was defiant. "Not guilty."

Blake opened a manila folder on the bench in front of him. "Your Honor, let the record show that I am tendering to counsel copies of all police reports, the coroner's report, police crime lab reports, report of DNA testing, copies of the crime lab photographs, and the defendant's criminal history sheet."

"Your Honor," Stan said, handing a written motion up to the judge, "at this time we'll move to request the State to turn over the actual specimen used to conduct the DNA test. We will be running tests of our own."

"Have you seen this?" The judge held up the motion to Blake.

"Actually, no, but we have no objection."

"Your Honor, we'll have our lab pick up the evidence directly, for chain of custody reasons."

"That's between you two. Anything further?" the judge asked.

"Not at this time, Your Honor."

Later that afternoon we sat in Stan's office, taking turns reading the documents. One thing in a supplementary report made me uneasy, a witness we didn't know about. In addition to Mr. Bonnerly, another man who lived across from the building also reported seeing Justin standing in front of the abandoned building, talking to the African male.

Lab reports confirmed that there were unidentified prints on the scooter; I had no doubt they were Akibu's, if ever we could get a comparison.

Reading over the medical examiner's report, I was struck by something odd. It described every wound in painstaking detail, but made no mention of any injury consistent with sexual violation. Still, he noted "a trace of dried white substance on the right buttock which proved, under microscopic examination, to be semen containing non-motile sperm."

"I'd like to talk to the medical examiner," I said. "Something's not right here."

"Call him now."

"Think he'll talk to me?"

Stan shrugged. "He's a public servant, and this is a public record. Tell him you're me. Tell him it will be easier to talk over the phone for a minute than making him appear for his deposition."

I called the coroner's office, asked for Deputy Coroner Sobczak. Luckily, he was in. I explained why I was calling; he didn't seem to mind.

"Doctor Sobczak, you make no mention of any trauma which might have been the result of sexual assault. A boy that age—if there had been anal penetration, there'd be an injury, wouldn't there?"

Stan had an old Regulator clock on his office wall. I listened to it ticking. For a moment I felt I'd put the doctor on the spot, but then he said, "Yes, I believe there would be. So what's your point?"

"If there was anal trauma, you would have noted it?"

"Yes, I would have noted it. There was no anal trauma. I do not believe there could have been penetration. Is there anything else?"

"No, thank you, Doctor." I started to say goodbye. "Wait, yeah, one more thing. Your report says there was a trace of what turned out to be semen. You specifically said *trace*. Does that mean—"

"Please wait, I need to get my own copy of the autopsy report." Sounding a little irritated, he put the phone down. Then he came back, said, "Okay. It says, quote, a trace amount of dried substance, end quote. So now what's your question?"

"The word *trace*, that would mean a very small amount?"

He sighed. "Yes. Trace means a very small amount."

"If there were, say, a normal amount of semen—whatever that is—you wouldn't have used the word *trace*, would you?"

"No," he said with exaggerated patience, "because then it wouldn't be a trace, would it?"

I hung up and stared at a stack of papers on Stan's desk. "What is it?" Stan finally asked.

"Something's not right," I said. "I just wish I could get a handle on it."

When I got home that night, Fred, my landlord, met me

in the vestibule on the first floor.

"There was a guy here asking for you today, a black guy," he said. "Wanted to know how to get in touch with you. I gave him your office number and address. I hope that's okay."

"Sure," I said, flipping open my mailbox. "Did he say what he wanted?"

"Not really, except that he was sorry he missed you. Said he had some kind of business with you."

There was no mail in the box. "Was there a mail delivery today?"

"Yeah, I got mine."

"This guy, did he come before or after the mailman?"

He pinched his chin, thought a moment. "After, 'cause I took my mail when the guy was leaving."

"What did he look like?"

"Black guy, about thirty-five, I'd say. Spoke with a foreign accent. Real polite."

A platoon of spiders crawled over my scalp. "He didn't say what he wanted?"

Fred looked at me like a kid who'd tried putting tin cans in the garbage disposal. "Geez, Mike, shouldn't I have give him your number? He acted like he knew you."

"It's okay, Fred. Thanks," I said. He went back into his apartment, and I stared at the empty mailbox.

CHAPTER TWENTY

Jail is a hard place. Hard walls, harder inmates, even harder correctional officers, and the corridors ring with the slamming of steel doors. Waiting for Justin in the visitors' area, I could not fathom a guy like him surviving in a place like this. I had no good news to bring him, but thought I could at least give him a little moral support. It was a shock when I saw him crossing the visitors' room in his orange jumpsuit. He sat down behind the glass, his eyes filled with a desperate, animal fear. I gave him a big, confident smile; he did not smile back.

"How's it going?" I asked.

He didn't answer, just lowered his head and shook it slowly, then gave me an anguished look. "How's Richard?" he asked.

I had no idea about Richard, but I couldn't tell him that. "Richard's okay. Beth is staying with him for the time being."

"She is?" Relief softened his face.

"Just for the time being. She's organizing some of your friends to help. Some social service agency wanted to put him in a nursing home, so that's why Beth is there."

He rubbed his knees, looking away. "Thank God. He can't go to a nursing home, not now." When he looked at me, his eyes were wet. "If only I could get out of here; I need to be with him now."

"Hang in there," I said. "Just hang in, we're working day and night." The words rang hollow in my ears.

His eyes unfocused a little then, and he smiled faintly at something inside his head. "Beth," he said. "Jesus, how

143

could you ever have given her up?"

Back at the office Stan Janda's voice, weary with resignation, spoke from the answering machine. "I need to talk to you." That was all he said, no hello, no goodbye. I punched in his number.

"We got the test results back from our own laboratory," Stan said. "The DNA's a match. If Canavan wouldn't consider a plea bargain before, he's really got Ambertoe by the shorts now. Nothing like proving the State's case for them, huh? I talked to Canavan today. They're going for the death penalty. No deals."

"Justin didn't do it, Stan," I said. "I know he didn't."

"Yeah, I know," he said, but there was no conviction in his voice.

I hung up and spun my chair to the window, a river of commuters flooding the sidewalk across the street heading for the train station. Was Stan really on board with this? I couldn't explain the DNA, but I knew Justin was innocent because I knew Akibu was guilty—why else would he go to all this trouble to scare me off? The bastard even killed poor Butler. He was dirty and now it was personal and I was going to fry the fucker.

I got my hat, went to the door, was about to shut off the lights in the reception area, when the phone rang again. I decided not to answer it. The answering machine clicked on, and Beth said, "Mike, are you there?"

I dashed back into my office and scooped up the phone. "Beth?"

"Mike, you never got back to me about the art fair. Are you coming?"

"Yeah, when is it?"

"When? Why, it's tomorrow."

"Tomorrow?" I mentally checked my schedule, though it had been a long time since I'd had a scheduling conflict.

"Yes, tomorrow." There was just an edge of irritation in her voice. "Didn't you get the flyer I sent you?"

"No. What time do you want me there?"

"Well, that's the thing. It starts at nine, and there's a lot to set up. Can you be here at seven?"

"No problem," I said, calculating that I'd have to get up before five. Then I began to wonder about the flyer. "Beth, was the flyer in an envelope?"

"Yeah, what else?"

"With your return address?"

"Of course, why?"

"Nothing."

"Mike, be sure to bring Stapler, okay?"

"It's Stapler you really care about, isn't it?" I said.

"Yes," she said. "Don't be late, there's a lot to do. Bye."

I drove home thinking about the flyer I didn't get, and with a jolt recalled the day Akibu showed up at my door, the day I got no mail. The thought released a bat in my stomach. Akibu knew about the art fair, and he knew where Beth lived.

I debated only a second whether calling her back might alarm her unduly, and called her from my apartment. I'd already told her about Akibu and poor Butler, and she wasn't easily spooked.

She picked up the phone before the second ring.

"I wasn't going to tell you this, Beth," I said, "but I'm pretty sure David Akibu stole the flyer from my mailbox."

"What makes you think that?" Her tone was mainly curious.

I told her about Akibu showing up at my door, about my

145

mailbox being empty that day.

"I'm glad you called. You're talking about a possibility; there could be other explanations. Don't worry about me, just watch out for yourself. See you in the morning—and don't be late, there's lots to do, okay?"

CHAPTER TWENTY-ONE

Next morning we were heading northwest on I-90, Stapler next to me with his paws on the dashboard, as the October sun rose behind us, igniting the cornfields with gold fire. This was bird-hunting season, what was supposed to be Stapler's season, but we hadn't gone hunting this year. If I didn't plan a trip now, the season would be over before I knew it. But with Justin locked up and that final gurney waiting for him to be strapped down, I found it hard to take even a single day off.

Poor Stapler. He's an artist's conception of what a bird dog is supposed to look like: noble head, long feathered tail that stands straight out when he's locked on point, one foot raised.

It is said that a dog's ability to point game is a refinement of the stalking instinct, honed through hundreds of years of breeding, to freeze the dog's behavior in the moment he is about to pounce. It so happens that those classic Currier and Ives poses are no longer in fashion among bird dog fanciers. Now the tail is supposed to stick straight up in the air like an antenna, and all four feet firmly planted on the ground. It is said that the raised foot is a sign that the dog is about to break.

I prefer the old fashioned look, but there is probably truth in the raised-foot business, because while Stapler looks the part, his behavior in the field leaves a lot to be desired. I've never seen a better dog when it comes to finding game birds. Trouble is, he just cannot hold point, cannot resist bolting before I can get into gun range—and sometimes he even captures the bird himself. On those occasions when he holds point perfectly, I know he is not on a bird, but rather a turtle or a frog or some dead animal—things he knows will not fly away.

So despite how handsome he is, a field trial specialist would brand him worthless, a waste of dog food. But every time he broke point prematurely, he never failed to show remorse afterward. He would come to me slowly, head hanging, with the sorrowful look of a drunk who'd once again fallen off the wagon, as though forgiveness were too much to ask. But there was always forgiveness. He just could not control his own impulsiveness. Besides, I had to admire the abilities he had. If the two of us were ever marooned on a desert island, it would be Stapler who would provide for us, catching birds and small animals. And without a doubt he'd bring them back to me, just as he always did. Stapler was trapped between his primitive canine world and the one into which he was supposed to evolve. A lot like me.

We nosed across the rusting railroad tracks into the corridor of elms arching over Sutler's Grove's Main Street, a town that had been blessed with two lives. It got started in the early settlement days as a trader's store, and grew into a farming community that prospered with the coming of the railroad. By the size of the abandoned train depot, the town must have hummed with commerce then, as the great Victorian houses grew up along its streets. But the railroad didn't stay, and though a pair of faded cross-bucks still guard the old rails, no train had passed this way in half a century. Route 14, slashing diagonally across country from Chicago, carried the commerce after that, bypassing Sutler's Grove by a mile. Its commercial arteries severed, the town withered on the vine.

Withered, but did not die. Out of the way, its grand old residences with adjoining outbuildings to be had for a song, it made a perfect haven for the artistically inclined; and a lot of imaginative paint schemes brought the town a whole new, if a little artificial, charm. Now it had the feel of a theme park—you expected that at any moment Mickey and Goofy and Snow White would come skipping down Main Street.

I made a U-turn mid-block. I didn't pull into the gravel driveway, which ran along the edge of Beth's property, thinking she'd want to set up tables there. I parked in front, the gingerbread facade of the old Victorian spotted with early sunlight, the small barn standing behind it like a shy calf with its mother. Before I cut the ignition, Beth was coming down the walk, beaming at me. Or I thought at me. She swung open the passenger door, wrapped herself around Stapler, who was caught up in a mania of face-licking, and I found myself terribly jealous of my own dog. Then she noticed that I was there, too.

"Right on time," she said, as I came around the car. She lifted to her tiptoes, kissed me on the cheek. It seemed so natural. I liked that.

At Beth's direction I carried a few long tables from the barn and set them up, forming an el on the driveway near the sidewalk and extending under the weeping willow that stood on the front lawn like a green mushroom cloud. All along the street, others were doing the same, setting out paintings and pottery, framed photographs and macramé, and the smell of bratwurst cooking drifted from the park at the corner where the nonresident artists were setting up booths.

"I'm only putting out the Kari pieces," she said, setting a cardboard box down on the lawn. When she stood, she put the back of a wrist to her forehead and stretched, her breasts rising enticingly against her green sweatshirt.

Beth had three artistic personas. She marketed her sentimental (kitschy) pieces, the ones that launched her into relative fame, under her own name: Maribeth Mahoney. She used pseudonyms for the other two styles: Heather Trail was the creator of the outdoorsy themes, while for her more abstract creations she used the single name, Kari. All of her signatures had one element in common: a circle dotted the *i*. The sentimental pieces—what she called her "commercial" pieces—sold mainly through catalogs and were the least expensive. The artsy, one-of-a-kind pieces brought the highest prices. In between was Beth's re-creation of the great outdoors, what I considered to be her best work: elk and moose and bear, loons, ducks, mergansers, eagles, owls. A duck hunter hopefully scanning the sky. Another one contented, poling a boat full of decoys and few dead ducks. And then there was my favorite, a handsome Llewellyn setter on point, an exact replica of Stapler.

But I was disappointed, as we went about removing pieces from boxes and arranging them on the tables and shelves, that my favorites were nowhere to be seen. "What, no wildlife?" I asked.

"I'm strictly Kari today," she said, pointing to the badge she'd pinned on her jacket, a little blue frame with the words 'Sutler's Grove Art Fair' and KARI in block letters. "It's an *art* fair, for Pete's sake. Which reminds me," she said. She rummaged in a cloth bag on the table, removed another badge. "Put this on," she said. It had my name on it.

"Why?"

"Because you're part of it. We're in this together." She laughed and took my hand, swung it twice and let it go, turning to open another box, and I was astonished at how that disarmed me, softened my knees and hardened my crotch, at how such a simple thing could seem so portentous.

"People will think I'm an exhibitor," I said. "What if they start asking me questions?"

"I'm sure you'll handle it."

When all the pieces had been set out, Beth went into the house and brought out a tray of coffee and bagels and cream cheese, and as we sat munching, awaiting the arrival of her public, I noticed, across the street and down one house, a couple of men in their late fifties in matching purple warm-up suits, hanging framed watercolors. From here it looked like they were all pastel flowers. When they finished, they sat down to partake of their own coffee and Danish, and when they spotted us they waved. Beth waved back. I smiled and nodded.

"See, now, George doesn't paint, he just helps Erik, but he's still wearing a badge. George is his life partner."

Did she put emphasis on "his"? *His* life partner? Just like us? A mixture of pleasure and angst rippled through my chest.

It was a perfect fall day, the smell of burning leaves in the air, the trees afire with color, lawns dappled with sunlight and fallen leaves. We passed the morning slouching in our lawn chairs, Stapler at our feet, thumping his tail at every passerby. He got almost as much attention as the artwork. With Beth all to myself, I was wishing the day could last forever. Beth smiled warmly at everyone. People would stop and heft the heavy bronzes, but when they turned them over and saw the prices, they'd quickly move on. Her least expensive piece, a fist-sized polar bear, was two hundred dollars.

"I really don't expect to sell anything," she told me in a brief interlude when we were alone. "It's just for fun. Just to be sociable."

But she did sell one piece, an abstract work that looked like a rising flame, for four hundred dollars. She seemed more surprised than I was.

After she'd taken the man's check, boxed the piece and sent him off, I said, "You hungry?"

"I could go for a brat. They smell terrific, don't they?"

I walked down to the food stand on the edge of the park, bought two brats, a couple of Cokes and a big bag of potato chips.

When I came back a young guy, skinny, white tee shirt and long, greasy hair, was looking over the shelves. I sat down, handed Beth a brat and a Coke, and started opening the potato chips. "How much is this one?" he said, tossing his hair out of his eyes, poking a finger at a statue of a nude. His arms were thin, his movements somehow uncoordinated. Now, looking at him more closely, I noticed a couple of fading turquoise half-moons under his eyes. He'd been clobbered pretty good. He didn't seem like the brawler-type—probably he'd just pissed off the wrong guy. And I was getting the feeling I'd seen him somewhere before.

"The price is on the base," Beth said. He picked it up and turned it over, exposing a tattoo on the inside of his forearm, but without looking at the price his eyes drifted to another piece. He put the nude back, then squatted, hands on his knees, to stare at a piece on the lower shelf. Something about this guy made me uneasy. Wherever I'd seen him, it didn't give me a good feeling.

"Did you bring any napkins?" Beth was holding a hand out, fingers spread.

"I'm sorry, what? Oh, no, I forgot."

"There's some in a cabinet in the kitchen. Would you mind?"

I went into the house, and in that old-time kitchen, which must have been the biggest room in the house, were about twenty cabinets. Most, I found, were filled with artists' supplies. I opened and closed doors, shifted contents to look behind things. I finally located an unopened package of napkins under the sink. I tore off the wrapper, and as I pulled out a dozen it hit me, the guy's tattoo, a heart and dagger: it was what Elmer Bumpp described on the guy with Akibu the night they delivered the hyena. He had to be the kid in the alley that night, the one who killed Butler.

I dashed for the front door, heart banging against my sternum, and swung it open. Beth's chair was empty. The guy was gone.

CHAPTER TWENTY-TWO

I scrambled down the stairs, and in my peripheral vision I caught sight of the two of them, standing on the lawn near the corner of the house.

Beth gave me a funny look. "Everything okay?"

I gave them my most ingenuous smile, holding the napkins aloft like a fisherman with a trophy trout, then walked casually over and handed them to her.

"This gentleman has an interest in old houses," she said. "I was just showing him around. Don't worry, I'm keeping an eye on the tables."

I turned to the guy, extended a hand. "Hi," I said, with a smile as big as a Buick. "I'm Mike."

He reached for my hand tentatively, his smile a little uncertain. I felt Beth's eyes on me. Instead of shaking his hand, I lay my hand over the back of it, gripped the outer edge, then twisted it up; and, as he bowed to ease the pain, I switched hands, slid my other hand to his elbow, and pinned his arm under mine. Now we were standing side by side, his arm couched in mine, his hand bent backward in my grip. Just by bending it a little and twisting it, I could inflict a lot of pain. His arm was so skinny, I thought it might break. He resisted only a little.

"Ow, ow, OW!" he said.

I applied a bit of pressure. "Shut the fuck up or I'll break it," I whispered. "We're going to take a little walk in the park, just you and me."

"Yeah, okay, Jesus, can you ease up?"

Beth just looked at me, her eyes a little wider than usual, her expression saying only that she hoped I knew what I was doing.

We walked side by side down the block, the bones of his wrist seeming no bigger than a woman's. I looked into his eyes. "Smile, for Christ sake," I said, and turned up the pressure. He made an *O* with his mouth and tried to stand on his toes; then I relaxed my grip a little and he smiled back.

"That's better," I said. Actually I didn't think his smile was all that genuine, but no one seemed to take any notice.

That is, until we passed Erik and George in their matching warm-up suits across the street. Erik nudged George. They both looked over. I patted the guy's hand and smiled over at them, and the two of them smiled back and nodded their approval. I was just glad it was an art fair, and not a rodeo.

We took a seat on a park bench. "I think you broke my wrist," he whined. "Please, ease up, okay?"

"Let's just talk," I said.

"All right, but let me go, it hurts like a motherfucker. I won't try to get away, I promise."

"What are you doing here?"

"I promise I'll just sit here; just let me go first, then I'll talk."

I tightened my grip. "Ow, ow, ow," he said. "Okay, okay. David sent me."

"To do what?"

"Just get the lay of the land."

"Lay of what land?"

"Just, you know, watch you and report back."

"You killed my neighbor's cat. Why?"

"Your neighbor's cat?" His eyes waxed thoughtful. "I

155

didn't kill the cat, David killed it. I wouldn't do that."

"What's the story with the hyena?"

"What hyena?"

I put a little pressure on his wrist. "Ow, *OW,* okay!" I eased off.

"The hyenas were supposed to be bred, right?" I said. He nodded.

"To be killed for *muti?*"

His eyes latched onto mine. "Killed? See, you don't know nothing, man. Do you know anything about a hyena? A hyena is your most sacredest animal; you know that? A hyena is totally supernatural, from the underworld. It's got, like, special powers."

I couldn't help snickering a little.

"Hey, laugh all you want, man, but do you know that a hyena can actually see the future?"

"And you learned this from David Akibu?"

"I learned it—" His eyes flicked off mine. "Yeah, from David Akibu. The guy's like a genius, you know? No, not a genius. The guy's a god."

"And you do whatever he tells you?"

"Hey, you don't know him, man. The dude's like, super-human. He's got powers; he can do magic and shit. David's like the African Jesus, you know? It's totally spooky. He came here to save African-Americans after four hundred years of oppression; you know that? Fuckin' racism in this country, outta sight, man. It's about time African-Americans had a savior, don't you think? Hey, could you just loosen your grip a little? It really, really hurts, man."

"Keep talking. Tell me more about David."

"Okay, okay. David's like Moses, see."

"I thought you said he was like Jesus."

"Jesus, Moses, he's a messiah, man, only he's like,

bringing Africa to black people instead of, you know, the other way around. Bringing the African-American the culture this country stole from him. Fuck reparations, man, this whole thing's way bigger. Way bigger than you know, it's fucking unbelievable."

"You call this guy a black savior, and he kills black children?"

"Hey, I don't know nothing about killing children, man, that's what you say. And anyways, I'm not into getting all judgmental, okay? The dude's like, like . . . Fuck, man, could you lighten up? It really hurts."

"Where can I find him?"

"Look, have a little pity. My wrist, it hurts like a motherfucker, man. I think you broke it." Tears were welling up in his eyes. "Just let me go." His voice was breaking. "I'll sit here; I won't try to get away, I promise. I swear on my mother's grave I'll just sit here."

I let him go. He sat there red-faced, rubbing his wrist a minute, then flexed it slowly.

"You got the guy all wrong, man. Like Abraham in the Bible. You know about Abraham? God told Abraham to burn his kid in a fire. You don't go questioning God, dude."

His tone was turning self-righteous. "When David talks, it's like God talking. You don't know who you're fuckin' with, man. If I was you, I'd stay away, let it alone; there's still time for you, if you just drop this whole thing right now. He never did nothing to you. Just let him do his thing. Otherwise—" His eyes deepened with messianic fervor. "He'll smite you with the wrath of God, dude."

"You got a driver's license?"

"Yeah, course."

"Let's see it."

He turned, raising one buttock, reached for his back pocket. Then he leapt to his feet and bolted straight across the park. I jumped to my feet to go after him, took about three good strides and suddenly a hot knife of pain shot through my ankle, pulled me up so quickly I nearly fell. I hopped on one foot back to the bench and sat down, kneaded my ankle and watched him reach the street on the other side of the park and disappear around a corner. I stood up, tested my weight and hobbled back to Beth.

She didn't get up, just followed me with her eyes until I sat down. "Are you going to tell me what that was about?"

"That was Akibu's pal."

"How did he . . . ? Oh," she said. "Right, the flyer in your mailbox. What's going on, Mike? What's he doing here?"

"Akibu's trying to scare me off, and I'm afraid he may be trying to get to me through you. Beth, please, I want you to be careful, okay? If you see anything strange, or if you see that lowlife around here, call the police right away."

Just before the sun had set, a full moon, orange as a pumpkin and perfectly round, rose out of the park and climbed above the gathering shadows. We didn't talk much, packing the artwork away, carrying boxes to the barn. It had been a perfect day until the hippie showed up. Now the thought that I'd gotten Beth mixed up in this thing hung around my neck like an anchor.

As I stacked the last folding table against the barn wall, the smell of old hay and motor oil still rising faintly from the dirt floor, Beth waited at the door, her hand on the light switch. "I'd like to buy you a drink," she said; then her eyes creased into a pretty smile. "Then you can buy me dinner. Fair enough?"

At that moment I wanted to take her in my arms and hold her forever, and then she flipped off the light, and I just stood there looking at her form silhouetted in the doorway, her breasts, her thighs coated with pale twilight, a work of art such as I'd never seen.

"Mike—were you planning to stay out here?"

We went into the house and she made drinks and we sat at the kitchen table. "What a gorgeous day," she said. "You were a terrific help." She put her hand on my wrist, rocked it. "Thanks."

When she moved her hand away, I took her fingers. She smiled at me and I leaned to her lips, tried to kiss her, but she turned away. "Don't," she said, retrieving her hand. Then she gave me a friendly smile. "We've had a really good day. Okay?"

"Okay," I said, and sat back. "Beth, we need to talk about this hippie, this whole situation. I'm really sorry I got you involved in it."

She put her head back and laughed. "Come on, Mike. I should thank you for bringing a little adventure to Mayberry."

She was being good about it, but this was serious. "I don't know what these animals are capable of."

She leaned forward, hooking me with her eyes. "I'm not afraid. Look, I really, really like Justin. I know he's innocent, I just know it, and if I wanted proof, this creep coming around does it for me. Why is this Akibu guy so afraid you'll find him? He must be guilty of something. Why else wouldn't he just come forward? God, whenever I think of Justin, that poor man, I—you're all he's got, Mike." She gave me a bright smile. "You're my hero, you know that?"

"Do you have a gun in the house?" I asked, pretty sure she didn't. In the days of our marriage, Beth had only tolerated my affinity to firearms.

"No. You know I wouldn't know how to use a gun."

"What if I gave you one, showed you how to use it?"

"No, I don't want a gun around the house."

"How about a baseball bat?"

She chuckled. "No, I don't have one of those, either, but if you want to get me a Louisville Slugger, that would be great."

We left Stapler in the house and went to dinner at a Chinese place just outside of Crystal Lake, romantic, low light, candles on the tables, and I found myself for the second time in less than a month watching a candle flame sparkle in Beth's eyes, wanting her beyond what I thought were the limits of desire. I tried to bring up the subject of us, she and I, of getting together again, and my soul ached with the thought of it. Instead I talked about movies.

Afterward I walked up the front walk with her, but didn't go in. Stapler met us at the door, and we stood for a minute on the porch in the moonlight.

"Thanks again, Mike," she said finally, raised up on her toes and kissed my cheek.

Then she went inside. I walked to the car sick with the thought of her vulnerability, living here all alone, and as I pulled away, I remembered a gun in a rack behind the counter at Maxon's, a Stoeger reproduction of an old double-barreled coach gun with hammers. It was about the length of a Louisville Slugger, and not much more complicated to use. I resolved to stop in tomorrow. If it were still there, I'd buy it for Beth.

I took Route 14 all the way into the city. The full moon had climbed high and shed the drama of its rising, hanging up there now blanched and shrunken, and mocking the erratic course of my life.

I could not approach Beth with the subject of getting together again because I still did not believe I could remain faithful to her. That was part of it, but it was enough. And the other part? This: *You could not bear the pain if, once and for all, she said no. You could not remember a time when you yearned more for her touch than you did tonight. But how can you be sure it just wasn't one more attack of hormones? Suppose she had satisfied that. Where would your head be then?*

CHAPTER TWENTY-THREE

It was eleven o'clock when Stapler and I got home. I took him for a short walk, and then I went to my filing cabinet and retrieved the *muti* articles I'd printed from the Internet, found the name of the Johannesburg detective who'd been quoted: Dieter Braacht, occult crimes section.

The fact that a unit was devoted to occult crimes was encouraging. To someone like Braacht, I might not seem the sort of guy who sees flying saucers. I pulled down an atlas from the bookshelf, determined that Johannesburg was eight time zones ahead—it would be seven-thirty in the morning there.

I got the number from international directory assistance, reached the Johannesburg Police Department, asked for the occult crimes section.

"There's no one there now, sir." She was polite, her accent that peculiar mixture of British and Dutch that is Afrikaans.

"Can you tell me, does Dieter Braacht still work in the unit?"

"Just a minute, I have to look in the directory." She came back ten seconds later. "Occult crimes," she said. "Here it is. Yes, Sergeant Dieter Braacht. He's the unit commander. I think they start at about nine o'clock."

I called back at one a.m. my time, reached the unit. "Sergeant Braacht," the man said. And suddenly I was overwhelmed by the seeming folly of what I was about to say.

"Hello?" he repeated.

My face burned with the realization that I couldn't begin to explain it all over the phone. I hung up.

Before going to bed, I let Stapler out in the yard. Since the night I found Butler mutilated, I rarely let him out alone. I'd stood at the porch railing in the light from the bare bulb, thinking that if I was going to talk to Braacht, it would have to be face to face. Thankfully my passport was current. I'd call Julia Ambertoe and tell her I needed to go to South Africa, and book a flight as soon as possible. It seemed the only thing to do.

The moon was up and the autumn air clear as ice, and in the pale light I could see Stapler chewing at something in the grass. He lowered his head and rubbed his neck and shoulder on the ground, then went back to chewing. I yelled to him. "Stapler, no! Come!"

He rolled upright, snatched up whatever it was from the grass and romped to the stairs. When he rose into view, what looked like a piece of rope was hanging from his jaws. He came to me and sat, ears forward, tail thumping, offering it to me, and suddenly, the vile odor assaulting my nose, I saw that it wasn't a rope but a dead snake dangling from his mouth, maggots dropping from it like grains of rice.

CHAPTER TWENTY-FOUR

I put the snake in a plastic garbage bag and carried it down to the trash, then I gave Stapler a bath in the basement laundry tub, the anger that had boiled into my neck still heating my face as I scrubbed him, wondering when they put the snake in the yard, how long it had been there. They could have poisoned Stapler just as easily. I didn't understand it. Maybe they thought killing him would just strengthen my resolve while, this way, they could wear me down one little terror at a time. Well, they were half right.

Now, I was going to kill this fucker.

I knew I wouldn't be able to sleep. When I finished with Stapler, I slipped on the gloves and went to work on the heavy bag that was hanging in the basement, and when I was nearly exhausted from pummeling Akibu and his flunky creep, I thought I sensed someone standing behind me and I whirled. Fred was standing sleepily at the bottom of the steps in his bathrobe.

"Sorry, Fred, I didn't think I was making that much noise."

He didn't respond, just turned around and walked back up the stairs, and when I heard him shut the door I turned the lights out and went up the back way. I hardly slept that night.

The next morning I called the detective area from my office, asked for Henry Simms, the investigator who arrested Justin. The officer who answered said Simms was on the

164

street. I told him I had information about the Brockton murder. He said he'd have Simms call me. Simms called back within the hour.

"I'd like to talk to you in person," I said.

"You want to come by the station at, say, four?"

I told him I'd be there.

At three-thirty I walked over to my car at the La Salle Hotel Parking Garage and drove to Area Two Headquarters. As Chicago police stations go, it was fairly new, the first floor housing the district station, the second the area detective division. I mounted the stairs and told the man at the desk that Detective Simms was expecting me. He asked me to take a seat. I walked to the men's room instead, taking in all the computers and high tech stuff. How things had changed. The old Maxwell Street Station where I'd worked was a relic that had survived the Chicago Fire.

On the men's room wall, some witless patrolman had scrawled above the urinal, "This is where all the dicks hang out." Some things are timeless; and precious, too.

I walked back and was about to take a seat when Detective Simms came up the stairs, suit coat slung over his shoulder. He was black, six-foot-three, square-jawed, neat mustache and intelligent eyes. He was followed by a white guy, red hair, at least a decade younger. By the full-framed .357 magnum in Simms' armpit, I figured he'd been around awhile. For the last ten years, the official sidearm was a semi-automatic pistol, though the revolvers belonging to the older men were grandfathered in.

Simms introduced himself. "And this is Detective Swain," he said. I pegged Swain in his late twenties; a 9mm Sig Sauer sat high on his belt.

As they led me to an interrogation room, I sensed that Simms and Swain were not a regular team. Simms was obviously in charge. I did not remember seeing Swain's name on the case reports. We sat down, Simms across from me, Swain tilting his chair on two legs against the wall, and I told them that I'd been a homicide dick myself, then let them know that I was working for Stanley Janda, former deputy superintendent. Chances were, though, that not even Simms had come on the job before Janda left.

I told them what I'd learned about Akibu. Simms listened politely, nodding only now and again. Swain kept tapping his thigh, as though listening to some rock beat inside his head.

I laid it all out for them, how Akibu was seen hanging around the abandoned building about the time Reggie was kidnapped, about his threats against me when I tried to find him, the disappearance of Kimberly Price, the mutilation of my landlord's cat, the dead snake dropped in my yard.

When I explained about *muti*, that it was a kind of witchcraft, Swain grinned, rocked his chair forward and said, "Witchcraft?" He gave me a look I'd seen on young coppers a thousand times before: cynical, condescending, arrogant. Then his eyes darted to Simms, looking for approval. Simms ignored him.

"Witchcraft," I said, leveling my gaze at Swain, and he tilted his chair back again, smiling at something only he knew. I began to sense how ridiculous I must sound, and it made me want to punch Swain's smirk right through the wall.

"This Kimberly Price," Simms said when I finished, "you said she's missing. But how do you know she's missing? Has her family reported it?"

"I don't know," I said.

Swain snorted. Simms pretended not to notice.

"But I can tell you this," I said to Simms. "Your little

friend here better file down the points on his star."

I expected more of a reaction from the little puke, but it seemed to pass over his head, and his face was in search of an appropriate expression.

But Simms knew. He warned me with a quick frown and subtle shake of his head. Then he said, "Mike, I know you're trying to do everything you can to help your client. I admire that. No kidding, I really do. But let's be realistic. I think your loyalty to this guy has colored your judgment."

I glanced over at Swain. His face had reddened. He seemed to be studying something behind his eyeballs.

Simms went on. "Look at the plain evidence. We got your guy in the building at the time the kid is taken. We got—"

"You know," Swain interrupted, "there's a way you maybe can help your guy." I watched Simms' eyes for disapproval. If he had any, he didn't show it.

"How's that?" I said.

Swain was looking at Simms as he spoke. "Tell your guy to come clean about the missing girl—what's her name, Henry? Lawanda Henry—tell us where she is, maybe we'll talk to the State's Attorney about cutting him a break." Now his eyes shifted to mine. "But there's no guarantees. You probably know that."

"Yeah, I probably do, Swain," I said.

"As I was saying," Simms said, betraying a hint of exasperation, "we got Ambertoe's prints on the kid's scooter, and his photographs of the scooter—while he's swearing up and down he never went near that building. And now we got his DNA on the dead kid."

"Not to mention your rump ranger's done it before."

I should have let it go. "Done what before?"

"He molested a kid in Texas. He's done hard time."

"Say you're back in homicide," Simms said, drawing me away from Swain. "Say you're me. Would you re-open the investigation?"

I looked at the table, gave it a couple seconds. The answer was depressingly clear. "Detective Simms, thanks for your time. I really do appreciate it. Just understand this. It doesn't end with Reggie Brockton. There's that missing little girl, and there will probably be more. This guy's going to do it again."

As I was getting up, Swain, his chair still leaned against the wall, said, "Witchcraft!" Then he raised two fingers and conducted his own version of the theme from "The Twilight Zone": "Doo-doo doo-doo, doo-doo doo-doo."

I hooked one foot under the leg of his chair and jerked it out from under him, and Swain slid down the wall and slammed onto the floor. He scrambled to his feet, and with the speed of a rattlesnake he swiped a sap from his back pocket, and then Simms stepped between us, seized my arm, threw me against the wall. I noticed from the corner of my eye, he was holding a restraining hand on Swain's chest. When Swain moved away, Simms handcuffed me behind my back.

"Go get an arrest slip," he said to Swain, then to me, "sit down."

I did. "Where do you think you are, man?" he said. When Swain left the room, he said, "I should've let him beat you into hamburger."

They left me sitting in there alone a long time, long enough to begin wishing I'd been nicer to Detective Swain, then long enough to wonder why I'd been congenitally denied the gift of calm reflection, and then I pondered whether Buddhism might hold an answer for me.

Simms came in alone and shut the door, sat across the

table from me. "I talked Swain into dropping it, although I'm not sure why I did that. At the moment he's my partner. You don't fuck with my partner."

I gave him the most contrite look I could muster. He uncuffed me.

When I reached the stairway, I spotted Swain standing at a copy machine, his lips drawn back in a kind of rictus, furiously chewing gum. I didn't think he saw me, but just as I started down the stairs he called out. "Duncavan!"

I turned.

"I think I know why you're trying to spring this fag, Ambertoe," he said, chomping through his smirk.

I was pretty sure I knew what was coming. "How's that?"

" 'Cause you like takin' it up the ass." His eyes brightened, the master of witty repartee.

"Ah, Swain," I said. "You clever boy. You will go far."

CHAPTER TWENTY-FIVE

I drove home basking in the warmth of my own virtue. I did not let Swain get to me that last time. I felt like calling Beth and telling her how I'd become a model of self-restraint. *You just don't get more emotionally stable than this, Duncavan.* But then I'd have to tell her all of it, how they'd nearly thrown my sorry Irish ass in jail. Maybe I should wait until I build a more impressive case.

Swain seemed awfully young to have made detective. The remark about filing down the points on his star had zipped right past him, an expression probably long abandoned. It was advice a more seasoned cop used to give to a cocky kid who, like Swain, thought his star was a license to abuse people. "File down the points on your star, son," we would say, " 'cause sooner or later someone's going to ram it up your ass."

The thought of Beth brought back a nagging worry about her vulnerability, and after dinner that night I drove out to Maxon's.

The coach gun was still standing upright in the rack behind the counter.

"Neat little gun," the guy said as he broke it open, handed it over to me. I closed the breach, swung it to my shoulder. Short, very handy. I cocked the hammers, then eased them down to be sure they could be lowered easily. I checked the markings on the barrels—twelve gauge, both barrels choked open. That meant maximum spread of buck-shot. With nine deadly balls exploding out of each barrel at once, you could not miss at close range. It was simple to operate, had none of the inherent dangers of an automatic pistol, and it was a lot more dangerous to a bad guy.

"I'll take it," I said. "And one box of double-0 buck-shot."

CHAPTER TWENTY-SIX

When I got to my office the following morning I called Julia Ambertoe in Texas.

"You want to go to South Africa?" she asked, her voice a little scornful.

"Johannesburg, to be exact," I said.

"Mr. Duncavan, you aren't 'junketing' by any chance, are you?" She emphasized the word.

"I won't even go, unless I'm sure I can talk to the right people first."

"That was just my little joke, Mr. Duncavan. If you must go, then go. Stop calling me. When your bills are too high, I'll let you know."

At midnight I telephoned Dieter Braacht in Johannesburg. "I'm an investigator in Chicago, working on a murder case, and I'd like to speak to you. I believe it was actually a *muti* killing."

His accent was Afrikaans, and his tone was wary. "You are with the Chicago police?"

"No," I said and added, "but I used to be. Now I'm a private investigator."

"And who are you working for?"

"Someone who's been accused of the crime. I strongly believe he's innocent."

He mulled that over. "I'm not sure what you want from me," he said warily.

"I'd like to talk to you, but not over the phone. I want to meet with you."

He hesitated. "You mean you want to come to Johannesburg?"

"That's right. I won't take up much of your time. It's just too important to discuss on the phone."

"I see no harm," he said. "When will you come?"

We set a date and time to meet at his office, and he gave me the address of the police station. When we were about to hang up, I said, "I would like to ask one question, if you don't mind. Does the name David Akibu mean anything to you?"

"Yes," he said. "Yes it does. Why do you ask?"

"I believe he may be the murderer."

"That's . . ." He seemed to gather his thoughts. "I'm afraid that's impossible, Mister . . . what did you say your name was?"

"Duncavan. Mike Duncavan."

"David Akibu is dead, Mr. Duncavan. His heart was cut out. He was the victim of a *muti* murder."

CHAPTER TWENTY-SEVEN

Dieter Braacht's final words sentenced me to one more sleepless night. What the hell was going on?

After my morning workout I called Beth, explained about the South Africa trip. "I'll be back in less than a week," I said. "Think I could drop off Stapler while I'm gone?"

"Sure," she said. "When?"

"I can come out tomorrow evening."

"I teach my ceramics class at the high school tomorrow. Could you come by in the afternoon?"

"I can be there about five," I said.

"Great. I think you are beginning to like Sutler's Grove."

"I bought you something," I said. "I wanted to give it to you before I leave."

"Oh? Am I allowed to ask what?"

"A coach gun. Know what that is?"

"No, I'm afraid I don't."

"Remember Kirk Douglas and Jimmy Stewart in *Cimarron Sundown*, when the undertaker wouldn't drive the horse-drawn hearse up to boot hill because the dead guy was a Mexican and the desperados say they ain't gonna have no Mexican buried in their cemetery, and they'll shoot down anyone who tries?"

"No, I don't think so."

"You remember—the Mexican's mother is crying and Kirk Douglas says, 'Don't worry, little lady, we'll take your boy up there,' and they climb onto the seat of the hearse and Jimmy Stewart drives these black horses with plumes on their heads through the crowd of bad guys while Kirk Douglas sits next to him with that short little shotgun across his lap?"

"I don't remember that."

"Sure you do, we watched it together. Then they pass by one particularly ornery-looking desperado who pulls a gun and tries to shoot Kirk Douglas in the back, but Kirk swings around and blows the guy away. Remember?"

"I never saw that movie. You must have seen it with someone else."

"Well anyway, that's a coach gun."

I drove Stapler through a light drizzle out to Sutler's Grove the following afternoon. When I pulled into the drive, I noticed the side door of the barn was ajar. I jangled the bell on the front door of the house; then when Beth didn't answer, I went around the back to the barn and knocked on the partially open door.

"Come on in," Beth sang from inside, and I pushed it open. She was working at a table in the center of the dirt floor, awash in the soft light from the high windows, a volume of the *World Book Encyclopedia* propped open on the table. Next to it stood a half-finished wax statue of a hyena, about a foot high.

"Interesting subject matter," I said.

"You like it?" Beaming, she wiped her hands on her denim smock. "It's for you."

"Beth, it's beautiful. So lifelike," I said. "And his expression is so—benign." The expression was almost friendly. It was uncanny how she'd captured that.

"It's a she," Beth corrected.

"Really. The detail is astounding, Beth."

"That's why I'm working in wax; I can get much more detail in wax than in clay." Her head was wrapped in a blue bandana and she brushed back a loose wisp of hair with the back of her hand. "You really do like it, Mike?" She raised her eyes to mine, checking if I really meant it. Her smile was disarming. She seemed as guileless and happy as a schoolgirl.

"I really do," I said.

"The subject matter—you probably think I'm crazy, but I started reading about them, and I thought, maybe we could sort of exorcise some demons. I mean, hyenas aren't really the vile creatures they're made out to be. And she's a mother; it's going to be a tableau, a pair of pups or kits or cubs or whatever they're called, on each side of her."

I noticed the lady came equipped like the mother of Romulus and Remus, ready to suckle her young. "You know about the genitalia?" I said.

She laughed. "Yeah, I read about that. Makes it easier for the sculptor to get it right, I suppose."

"Beth, it's absolutely magnificent."

"I'm going to do the casting myself." She'd had her own small foundry in the barn since the beginning, when she started selling her work. She used to turn out every piece by her own hand. But when the demand gave birth to a growing enterprise, she had to outsource the final casting to a commercial foundry. The original work was still all done by her own hand, though, and all were limited editions.

"One thing I read haunted me," she said. "An anecdote reported by a husband/wife team who were doing a field study of hyenas in Zimbabwe. Actually, it was what inspired me to do the tableau. Want to hear?"

"Sure."

WHAT THE HYENA KNOWS

"Well, these two naturalists had been observing a solitary female and her two pups. She had a burrow in the bank above a river, and the naturalists were recording her comings and goings, her interaction with the pups, that kind of stuff.

"Then one really hot and dry afternoon something odd happened. The mother took her pups in her mouth, one at a time, splashed across the river, carried them up a hill on the other side and disappeared into some underbrush.

"The naturalists didn't know what to do—whether they should move their blind or what. Since it was late in the afternoon, they decided they'd deal with it the next day.

"But that night a terrific storm came up, Mike. It was the middle of the dry season, completely unexpected. And the river rose and overflowed its banks, and the hyena den was flooded. It was under several feet of water."

"That's quite a story," I said.

"If they weren't responsible scientists, I wouldn't have believed it." Her expression shifted. "Where's Stapler?" she said, wiping her hands with a cloth.

"In the car, I'll get him. And the present I brought you, which I'm afraid is a little inadequate. It can't compare to yours."

When I opened the car door Stapler dashed past me and into the barn, and when I followed carrying the box with the gun, Beth was kneeling beside him, scratching his neck. I laid the box on the table next to the hyena. "Open it," I said.

She did, then stood, looking down at it without expression.

"Go ahead, pick it up."

She shook her head. "Is it loaded?"

I lifted it out, broke it open, showed her the empty bar-

177

rels. Then I showed her how to open it herself, how to drop a pair of cartridges in. "They don't generally make shotguns with hammers anymore," I said, "but I think it's a great safety feature—you've got to cock the hammers to fire it. And it's easy to see if it's cocked. Here," I said.

She took it tentatively, as though I was handing her a rattlesnake. I had her practice opening and closing the breach, throwing it to her shoulder, and cocking the hammers. Then I made sure she could safely let the hammers down, if necessary. Then I opened the box of shells, removed two, and showed her how to drop one into each barrel.

"I really wish you could practice shooting it," I said. "We'll definitely do that when I get back from Africa."

She gingerly set it down on the oiled paper in the box, and smiled at me with uncertain eyes. "Thank you, Mike. That is sweet, worrying about me. But I just don't think I'm a gun person."

"You ought to carry it around the house with you during the day, just to get used to the feel of it."

"We'll see," she said, and closed the lid of the box.

CHAPTER TWENTY-EIGHT

Three days later I drove to O'Hare, dropped the Omni in long-term parking, and flew to New York, then boarded a South African Airlines 747 for Johannesburg. It was a fourteen-hour flight, but in midweek it was less than half full, so I was able to stretch out across several seats, sleep through most of it, and arrive in reasonably good shape at two-forty p.m.—seven-forty a.m. Chicago time. My appointment with Dieter Braacht wasn't until the following morning. In the cab on the way to the hotel, I decided to take a detour, do a little sightseeing.

"Can you take me to a *muti* market?" I asked the driver.

He flicked his eyes to mine in the rearview mirror, grinning. *"Muti?"* His tone was skeptical. "You know what is *muti?"*

"Yes," I said.

"Not too many Americans go looking for *muti*. But I take you."

"Does *muti* work?" I asked.

He gave an exaggerated shrug. "Some say yes, some say no," he said, letting me know he was not one upon whom things were easily put over.

"What do *you* say?"

It took him so long to answer I thought he was ignoring me. Then his head began to bob slowly up and down and, as if he were speaking to someone inside his head, he said matter-of-factly, "It works."

"What about human *muti*," I asked. "Does it work?"

179

Suddenly his dark eyes were troubled. "What do you mean? There is no such thing as human *muti*." The scowl stayed. I dropped it.

He seemed to warm a little by the time he pulled over next to an outdoor market. "Do you want me to wait?" he asked.

"I'd like you to be my guide," I said. "We'll just leave the meter running."

There were vendors selling fresh produce and watches and tee shirts, and a few selling *muti*. Most were under canvas, though the first *muti* seller we passed had his wares spread on the ground: baskets filled with colorful powders, dried herbs, animal skulls, monkeys that looked as though they'd been freeze-dried. A little farther on we entered a tent with animal parts arrayed on tables, jars filled with colorful liquids, dried plants hanging from strings. The proprietor, a woman looking more Indian than African, was conversing with a customer, holding what looked like the jawbone of an animal, gristle still attached.

After listening a moment, the driver explained, "This woman has a child with a toothache. That is hyena, ah . . ." He ran a finger along his own chin. "The jawbone. The lady tells her to crush it into powder, very fine, and put it on the child's tooth."

I waited awhile, wanting to speak to the proprietor, but when the conversation didn't end, we moved on. The next vendor occupied a small hut, the smell of dead flesh mauling my nostrils as we approached. What looked like a hundred road kills dangled from the ceiling. "This man is a witch doctor," the driver whispered to me as we entered. He said something to the proprietor in Swahili. The proprietor smiled and nodded at me, apparently pleased at my interest.

"*Muti* works?" I asked, trying not to sound condescending.

He did not seem to take offense. "Oh, yes, it works. Strong medicine," he said, leaning across a row of dead baby crocodiles.

"What about human *muti?*"

His smile vanished, his eyes wary now. "I don't know about that," he said, his tone gone cold. "We do not use human *muti.*"

As we left, I thanked him and he nodded. His smile did not return.

The next morning, the toney shops along Johannesburg's main boulevard through the cab window reminded me of Chicago's magnificent mile, yet not a mile away witch doctors were selling magic herbs and animal organs. And maybe human organs. And it struck me: the same thing may already be happening in Chicago.

Dieter Braacht, about forty, slender, dark beard streaked with gray, dressed in a shirt and tie and a 9mm Glock on his belt, showed me to his small office. A two-foot-high wooden carving of an African tribesman stood on his desk next to his computer, draped with beads, very much like the one I'd seen in the market in Chicago.

I told him about the murder of Reggie Brockton, and about all the rest of it. I tried to give him every detail, and I didn't minimize the strength of the State's case against Ambertoe. He listened, nodding now and then. He had the alert calm of a psychotherapist. When I finished, he sat silently, a Bic pen held loosely with the point on the desk, running his fingers down the barrel, turning it over on its end and doing it again.

"So, what do you think?"

He leveled his eyes on mine, canted his head. "I think you have a *muti* murder," he said matter-of-factly, his crisp

181

accent lending authority to his opinion. "How can there be any doubt? Look, you have the killing of the child, the taking of the organs. You have this man who calls himself David Akibu near the crime scene, the name of a man who happened to be the victim of a *muti* killing. You have the woman who told you this man is involved in *muti*, a woman who's now disappeared. How much evidence do you need?"

Braacht had apparently forgotten that I was not the one who needed convincing.

"Will you tell that to the Chicago police?"

"If they ask me, of course, I will help in every way I can. But I haven't been asked." His face grew dark then. "Something else about this troubles me. You say another child has gone missing?"

"Yes," I said. "A girl. About a week later."

"It is possible that the girl is being kept alive. Until her organs are needed."

"Christ," I said. "Doesn't that make you want to get involved?"

"Of course it does. And that is up to you, to convince them to contact me. Listen, we need to talk more about this man who calls himself Akibu. Come with me; I want to take you to the village where Akibu was killed."

CHAPTER TWENTY-NINE

As we drove through the outskirts of Johannesburg, Braacht explained some of human *muti*'s gruesome details. "Human organs provide the most powerful medicine of all. The organs are cut out, dried and crushed for their magic. If you eat the brain, you will become smarter; eat the sex organs, you will become more virile. Bury a skull next to your shop, business will improve."

"But why children?" I asked.

"That is the biggest bonus you can get. Especially a young girl, still a virgin. The energy forces are the strongest, barely used, that's what they need. They will take a sacred knife used only for the purpose, one with a long blade. They will cut out the child's liver, the kidneys, while she is still alive. Because the more she screams, the more pain she endures, the more powerful the medicine's going to be."

We were traveling through open country, past fields of sugar cane and banana plantations, and came eventually to a scattered collection of tin-roofed huts. We parked the car and walked up a dirt street the color of ochre.

"This is the village where we found David Akibu's body," he said, nodding and smiling to onlookers, who eyed us curiously as we walked through the village. Then to me he said, "Akibu was an architect, a brilliant young man, about twenty-seven." The villagers seemed friendly enough, and I had the impression they liked Braacht.

He stopped at the door of a hut. "This was the witch doctor's hut, a man named Dwani Mwenyako, the man we believe killed David Akibu. He's wanted for Akibu's murder." We ducked under the low doorway. The back seat of a car was propped against one wall as a sort of couch. Braacht pointed to a place where the dirt floor had been dug up recently. "This is where we found Akibu's body. They only took his heart; they didn't harvest any other organs." Going back out into the sunlight, he said, "Feel free to talk to the people, if you like."

Across the sun-drenched street a couple of teenaged girls watched us from the front of a tin-roofed hut, then smiled shyly as we walked toward them. "This is my friend," Braacht told them, "a policeman from America, over for a visit." They nodded, their smiles brightening.

"Did you know the man who lived there?" I asked one of them.

She was still smiling, but her eyes shifted to the distance. She folded her arms, looked at her feet, gave a short, nervous laugh. She did not answer.

"Won't you talk to me?"

She laughed again, shaking her head. "It's too dangerous." She turned away, walked into the hut. The other girl followed.

I made eye contact then with a man about thirty-five in a Nike baseball cap standing nearby. He looked friendly enough. I asked him, "Why won't they talk to me?"

He shifted nervously, slipped off his hat, ran a hand over his head. "It is too dangerous." He turned and walked quickly away.

"You see what we're up against," Braacht said as we drove back to Johannesburg. "It's really, really hard to get witnesses to come forward. You saw the fear. They refuse to come to court, because they know that as soon as they testify, they will die."

Back at the police station, I asked Braacht if he could give me a photo of Mwenyako. He went to a filing cabinet, pulled out a copy of a police bulletin, handed it to me. It had his picture, with an inset of his fingerprints. He looked both younger and thinner than I expected.

"Is that the man you are looking for in America?"

"I've never seen him," I said. "But I'll bet it is. Can I have a copy of this?"

"I have several in the file. You can keep that one."

"Is it possible to speak to Akibu's family?" I asked.

He shrugged. "His mother lives here in Johannesburg. She's an elementary school teacher. I can give you her address." He wrote on a notepad. "I know it by heart," he said, tore it off and handed it to me. "Come on, I'll drive you back to your hotel."

In front of the hotel, I thanked him for his help. He shook his head. "It's you who've helped me," he said. "Now I know where Dwani Mwenyako is. Mwenyako has all of Akibu's identity papers. I'm going to go through regular channels, try to have him arrested on our warrant, but that will take time. And in any event, I don't know how that will help your own case. I'm sure the Chicago police are convinced they have the right man in that one. I can't say that I blame them."

I was opening the car door to get out, but his last remark prompted a question. "I know," I said. "The semen on the child's body—do you have any idea how to explain that?"

He looked at me, mulling it over. "Offhand, two things come to mind. First, as a disinterested observer, how could I rule out the possibility that your client *is* involved? That he somehow collaborated in the murder?"

"Right," I said, sorry I asked. Then, when he didn't go

on, I said, "What's the other possibility?"

He stared at me. "Don't ever underestimate him," he said levelly. "Don't ever forget that you are dealing with a witch doctor—a true *sangoma*."

That evening I took a cab to see Akibu's mother. She lived in a residential neighborhood of quiet streets and single-story residences much like a suburb of Chicago, in a small yellow house behind a low brick wall topped with ornamental iron.

She invited me in, a heavyset woman about forty-five, with kindly eyes. I told her I was investigating a *muti* killing in Chicago, and that I thought the murderer was the man who killed her son.

She stared, her eyes gradually comprehending. Then she said, "I only hope you catch him. He is evil. A dangerous man."

"Do you know how your son happened to come in contact with him?"

"No. David had his own apartment. On the night he died, he went out to a club. He met some friends there. That was the last time he was seen alive." Her eyes grew wet. "David was a brilliant young man. Brilliant. The hope of Black Africa."

"What can you tell me about *muti?*" I asked.

"It is a way of life. Go to any village, you will find witch doctors—*sangomas,* they are called—they prescribe ancient remedies, summon spirits," she said. "Usually, it is harmless, it does not involve humans. Now David, he was ashamed of such things. It embarrassed him; he thought it made Black Africans appear backward. He never took it seriously, that is the irony. Because it killed him."

When I said goodbye, she said, "I hope you can let me

know what happens somehow. David was my only child. When he died, my own life ended."

I didn't sleep on the flight home. I sat with my face close to the window, staring into the blackness, suspended in the ether and helplessly imagining Lawanda Henry, the missing girl who might still be alive, all alone in some dark room. Waiting to be slaughtered.

CHAPTER THIRTY

I mounted the stairs to my apartment, jet lag hanging on my shoulders like a side of beef. There was a message from Beth on the answering machine: "Call me whenever you get in. It's important." Her words seemed dipped in gloom. I decided to put off calling her until I got some sleep but, after collapsing into bed, I lay awake pondering the possibilities. I got up, dialed her number.

"I'm afraid I have some bad news," she said. "Richard died this morning."

I tried to process what she was telling me through the fog in my head. "Who?"

"Justin's Richard?" she said. "God, poor Justin. Do you think there's any possibility they might let him attend the funeral?"

"I'll talk to Stan Janda. But no, I don't think so."

"You're going to have to break the news to him, Mike."

"Why me?"

"I don't think it should come from his lawyer."

"You could visit him, you know."

"I can't do it, Mike. You have to."

"He's got other friends. Why does it have to be me?"

"Because it just does. None of his friends have visited him at the jail."

"You have."

"I can't, Mike."

"His friends can start now."

"Mike, please. Will you do this for me?"

The next morning I called Stan Janda from my office, told him the whole story—about everything I'd learned in Johannesburg. He listened without comment. When I finished, all he said was, "Holy shit."

"I don't know where we go from here, Stan," I said. "I doubt it will make any difference to the prosecution."

"Our only chance is to find this Akibu. Or whatever his name is."

"As far as I'm concerned, his name is David Akibu. If we're going to find him, that's the name he's using." I didn't say it, but even if I found him, what could we prove?

I told Stan, then, about Richard's death, told him I'd drop by the jail and break the news to Justin that afternoon.

"Christ," he said. "It's gonna kill him."

"You think there's any chance of getting him out, just for the funeral?"

"You think the Reverend Farrakhan might be the next pope?" That didn't call for a response. Then he said, "Mike, maybe we should try talking to Canavan anyway. I mean, about this African guy, this ritual killing. What do you think?"

"You're the lawyer." I had an idea where this was going. He seemed to want me to call Canavan, to trade on my friendship, and I didn't like it. Worse, as a non-lawyer I had no business discussing Ambertoe's case with the prosecutor.

I waited for Stan to respond. When he didn't, I said, "You're asking *me* to call him?"

"You know the guy pretty well; it might be better coming from you."

"I'm not a lawyer," I said.

"What can it hurt?"

My pride, my friendship, my self-respect—those were a few things off the top of my head.

When I didn't respond, he said, "Mike, I don't have to tell you we got a life hanging in the balance here."

"All right, I'll call him," I said.

I went to the jail intending to tell Justin about Richard first thing, so it didn't seem to come as an afterthought—*Oh, by the way, Richard's dead.*

But I changed my mind. Time was running out, and we had more serious business to discuss, and I was afraid that the news of Richard's death would put an end to any more conversation this day.

I watched him cross the room to the table, his cheeks more hollow since the last time I saw him. Before he even sat down behind the glass, he asked anxiously, "How's Richard doing?"

I ducked the question. "I want you to look at this," I said, and showed him the Johannesburg police bulletin, the picture of Dwani Mwenyako. "Do you recognize this guy?" He stared at the picture for several seconds, then looked at me confused, a little wide-eyed. "Yeah, that's him. That's David."

It gave me no sense of triumph. It was something I already knew, and now the duty of telling him about Richard weighed in my gut like a lead sinker.

"Justin, I'm afraid I have to give you some bad news." That was the left hook, to be followed by the right cross. I gave it a couple of seconds before delivering the blow. It was unnecessary.

His lips parted, his cheeks colored. "Richard?" he said.

I nodded. "I'm really sorry, Justin."

His expression didn't really change, but his face seemed

190

to turn to wax, solidify. The color drained away, his lips grew rigid, transparent. Then he stood without a word and walked away.

Richard's funeral service was held on a sunny October day in Rogers Park, a neighborhood of tree-lined streets and green lawns, at an Episcopal church that looked like a church ought to look, its gothic walls clad in ivy, the edifice drawing dignity down from the sky. I sat near the back with Beth. She remained composed until, halfway through the Mass, the bell began its mournful toll, and then she pulled a handkerchief from her purse and dabbed at her eyes.

There were refreshments afterward in a church meeting room. On a plain table stood a solitary picture of Justin and Richard standing above a blue-green sea in Yucatán, Justin's arm draped over Richard's shoulder, both of them looking very happy. Most of the guests seemed to be from the gay community, and I gathered from their conversation that the angel of death was a familiar visitor in their midst.

It was after three o'clock that afternoon when I got to my office, dreading the task I could not put off. I dug out my black telephone directory and found Blake Canavan's number at the State's Attorney's office.

"Mike," Blake said when he answered, "what can I do for you?" Upbeat, yet deferential. Back at the old firm I had to pry him away from calling me "Mr. Duncavan."

"There's a whole lot I've found out about the Brockton murder, Blake. Can I talk to you?"

His hesitation was so brief I may have imagined it. And maybe I imagined, too, the guarded edge that now came into his voice. "Yeah, but—Stan Janda knows you're talking to me?"

"Yes, he does." I resisted telling him it was Stan's idea. "Can I drop by your office? I've uncovered some pretty strange stuff. Might be better if I could meet with you in person."

This time the hesitation was obvious. "Mike, you know there's not a lawyer around that I have more respect for, but I just don't know . . ." He wanted to weigh his words now. "I can't do you any favors, Mike."

I felt my face flush. "Favors? God *damn* it, Blake, you think I'm looking for a favor? You think I'd actually do that?"

The line was silent for several heartbeats, and when he spoke his tone had softened. "All right, Mike, I'm sorry. But it might be better if we just talk on the phone, okay?"

"For Christ's sake, Blake, forget about Justin Ambertoe for a minute. We've got a fucking killer out there. You can bet he took that little girl, and you know what? She could still be alive, waiting to be executed, and nobody's doing a damn thing about it."

When he didn't say anything, I started feeling foolish, and felt more so when he responded, his calm manner in stark contrast to my own. "Sorry, Mike. I wouldn't say nobody's doing anything about it. That's an ongoing investigation. You want to tell me, uh, what you called about? I've got plenty of time."

I laid it all out, except for the hyena in the park. Akibu hanging around the building the night Reggie Brockton was kidnapped. Akibu's desperate attempts to keep me from finding him. I told him about the *muti* murders in South Africa, the ritual killing, how the removal of the organs explained the mutilation of Brockton's body. And I told him that the little girl could be alive, waiting like a lamb in a slaughterhouse.

"Well, that's quite a story," he said, and had it been anyone else I would have thought I was being patronized. He paused for several seconds. "Mike—why are you telling this to me?"

"Because no one is looking for this fuck. No one but me."

"You've got to take that up with the police. You know that."

"I already talked to the police. They won't listen to me. They'll listen to you."

He laughed. "They won't listen to me; I'm just an Assistant State's Attorney."

"Then go to the State's Attorney."

"You think O'Meara listens to me? The office just doesn't work that way."

"He'll listen to you more than he'll listen to me."

He seemed to mull that over. "Okay, Mike. If it was anyone else asking, I wouldn't—"

"Don't do this as a favor to me, Blake. Do it because it's the right thing to do, because it might save a little girl's life."

When he was silent again, I thought maybe I'd gone too far. Then he spoke, his tone resigned. "Okay, I'll talk to him and get back to you."

I hung up, an unsettled feeling rumbling through my gut. I turned my chair to the window and stared at the traffic stacking up at the light on Wells Street. I had a feeling I'd bargained away something of value, and there would be nothing to show for it.

After dinner I fed Stapler, let him out in the yard, and sat down to watch the evening news. There was a story about the still-missing girl, Lawanda Henry, some witless reporter sticking a microphone into her mother's face as she was getting into her car. "How do you feel, Mrs. Henry?" the reporter asked.

The phone rang just as the program broke for a commercial, and the idiotic question—"How do you feel, Mrs. Henry?"—was still echoing in my head when I picked up the receiver.

"This is David Akibu," the baritone voice said. "I understand you are still looking for me." Pinpricks crawled up my arms.

"You could make it a whole lot easier," I said. "Just tell me where you are."

"I warned you. You have no business with me."

"Then what are you afraid of?"

Laughter roared out of him like a stick banging the inside of an oil drum. "I fear nothing, Mr. Duncavan. It is you who are afraid of me. You have learned something of my power."

"Do you have a regular job, or do you just call up people and annoy them?"

"I am a missionary," he said. "Your white missionaries stole the African's religion. I'm here to give it back. And when the white man dragged the African from his homeland, they separated him from his soul. The black man may have won back his freedom. Some of it. But never his soul. I, David Akibu, bring the soul of Africa to the black American."

"No shit?" I said, because I couldn't think of anything better to say.

"Such a brave front you put on, Mike Duncavan, pretending you do not fear me. Of course you fear me. You know that I can go into your head, see your thoughts. Do you remember dreaming of me?"

A chill rippled up my neck. "Why don't you find yourself a Dumpster somewhere and stand in it? Then I'll come by and we can talk a while before they carry you away." If I could keep him talking, he might let something slip, some clue that might help me find him.

He chuckled. "You do not want to meet me, I assure you. I warned you once. I can control you, make you do things."

"Then meet me. Show me."

"Show you?" he laughed again. "Very well. In less than a minute, you will put the phone down and you will run away in a panic."

"See now, that doesn't count. I do that all the time. Where's Kimberly Price?"

"Do not worry about Kimberly Price."

"Tell me where she is."

"She does not want to see you."

"She can tell me that herself."

"You used to have a very handsome dog," he said. "Whatever happened to that dog? English setter, wasn't it?"

It struck me like a crack in the face. Where the hell was Stapler? I'd let him out in the back yard nearly an hour ago, forgot to let him back in.

I dropped the phone, my scalp crawling with visions of Stapler strung up like Butler. I ran to the back door.

"Stapler," I called from the porch. He was not in the yard. "Stapler!"

And then he was at the bottom of the stairs, scurrying up the steps.

I went back to the phone. "Listen, you fuck . . ."

Akibu's voice dripped with amusement. "You are back already?"

"I know you're in this country illegally, and sooner or

later you'll be caught. And I know you aren't David Akibu."

"But I *am* David Akibu. How little you understand of the true religion—it is quite the opposite of yours, Mr. Duncavan. So blinded by Christianity, you cannot begin to comprehend the most fundamental things. You were an altar boy once, weren't you, Mike Duncavan?"

"Where's the little girl?"

"St. Gabriel's, wasn't it? Even went to seminary for a time."

My stomach wrenched. How could he know that? "Listen you maggot, tell me what you did with that little girl."

"At your Mass, the priest turns bread and wine into the body and blood of Jesus Christ. And then you drink Christ's blood and you eat his flesh, do you not? Transubstantiation, I believe you call it?"

"Fuck you." I was losing it. "I know who you are and I'm going to find you, so why not just cut the bullshit and meet me somewhere?"

"But you don't know who I am." He gave a patronizing chuckle. "You only think you do."

"You're Dwani Mwenyako, quack witch doctor, lowlife shit with the soul of a hyena, and it's only a matter of time until I get you."

"You compliment me, Mr. Duncavan. The hyena knows things of the cosmos you can never begin to comprehend. I am David Akibu. David Akibu is me. I became him through transubstantiation—I ate his heart." He gave a low, rumbling laugh. "And soon I shall eat yours."

I sat on the couch for a long time scratching Stapler behind the ears, those final words echoing in my brain like a bad tune, and a sense of helplessness covering me like a blanket of nettles. I went to bed. A lot of time passed before I fell asleep.

CHAPTER THIRTY-ONE

The phone rang again about three in the morning. I snatched it up; sure it was Akibu again.

"Mike?" It was Beth, her voice high-pitched, frightened. "I think I just shot someone."

I sat up, coming full awake. "Jesus, what . . . ? Are you okay?"

She was weeping softly. "Yeah, but I'm scared to death." Her voice shook. "Someone broke into the barn."

"Did you call the police?"

"Yes," she said. "They aren't here yet."

"You're sure you're okay?"

She sniffled. "Yeah. I just wish they'd get here."

"How long ago did you call?"

"It was just, maybe five minutes ago."

"Are you in any danger?"

"I don't think so." She paused, and with a little more control she said, "No, I'm okay."

"Listen," I said, "just take your time and tell me what happened."

This is what she told me. It had started to rain about the time she went to bed, and a wild storm grew up during the night. Twice she was awakened by the wind whipping sheets of rain against the window.

Then something else woke her, she wasn't sure what, and she sat up listening, and heard what she thought at first was the rumble of distant thunder. Then, her face hot with fear, she realized it wasn't thunder at all. Someone was sliding the barn door open.

She threw on a robe and went downstairs as quickly as she could in the darkness, pushed aside the curtain in the kitchen window and saw the opening in the barn's main door, exposing the black maw of the interior.

Heart pounding, she went to the phone on the kitchen wall, punched in the illuminated numbers for the county sheriff's office and told the dispatcher there was a burglar in her barn.

She hung up and, as she stood there in the kitchen waiting for the police to arrive, the knowledge that the barn contained every piece of sculpture she owned began to steel her with anger. Now she looked out the window again. A flash of lightning lit up the barn's interior. She saw a dark figure standing inside.

Her eye fell on the shotgun propped in the corner. She stood motionless with indecision; then her eye drifted to the box of shotgun shells atop the refrigerator. She took down the box and loaded the gun with two cartridges. Then she went outside, onto the back porch.

She drew an involuntary breath as the icy rain hit her, drenched her face and soaked her bathrobe. The plunging branches of the willow tree fractured the light from the street lamp, sent wild shadows chasing across the lawn. She walked down the steps slowly, then across the yard and stood to one side of the gaping doorway. She cocked both barrels.

"Who's there!" she called.

There was no sound but the steady hiss of wind-whipped rain. She held the gun in her two hands with the stock pressed to her side, blinking rain from her eyes. Then for an instant she released one hand to push back a strand of wet hair plastered to her face, and in the same instant a hooded figure came out of the barn with his head down, advancing on her, a long object in one hand.

"Stop," she screamed, and in that split second, her knees seeming about to melt, she knew that she could not shoot him. He was still coming, was nearly upon her, and she pointed the muzzle above his head and fired, and the man's arms flew up and he collapsed backward and lay very still. His face was turned away from her, one cheek resting in the mud. Rain was soaking his sweatshirt.

Weeping, she threw the gun to the ground and drew closer to the body and stood peering down at him.

Now the man sat up abruptly, grabbed for her ankle. She pulled away, and then he scrambled in the mud toward the gun, but Beth was closer and she snatched it up, and now he rolled away, leapt to his feet and bolted around a corner of the barn. She did not follow.

Her voice was calmer, now. I waited for her to go on, and when she didn't, I said, "You think you'd recognize him, if you saw him again?"

"No. I never saw his face."

"Did you see any blood?"

"I didn't look. And anyway it was too dark. Mike—do you think it was that creep who was at the art fair?"

"I don't know," I said, guilt coursing through my veins like acid. "I'm just glad you had that gun."

"He didn't seem afraid of the gun; he just came right for me."

"He probably didn't see it until you fired."

"God, I aimed over his head, then I was so sure I shot him. Do you suppose he's wounded?"

"I doubt it. With that gun at close range, you'd either

kill him or miss clean. You probably caused him to load up his pants, though."

"Well, honestly I'm relieved he's not dead." She paused. "The police just pulled up, Mike. I should go."

"Beth, don't mention anything about shooting at the guy."

"No? Are you sure?"

"Yeah, they just might make you out to be the bad guy. Some cops get real paranoid about non-cops and guns. When the guy came toward you, did you see what it was he had in his hand?"

"No."

"Then definitely don't tell them. Do you want me to come over?"

She didn't say anything for a couple of seconds. "No, don't be silly, it's too far." I thought she was hanging up, but then she came back on. "Could you, please, Mike?"

CHAPTER THIRTY-TWO

In twenty minutes I was dropping change in the basket at the first toll plaza on I-90. I set the cruise control at eighty-five, hoping the state police would be elsewhere in these wee hours.

By the time I got to Sutler's Grove the rain had slowed to a drizzle, and Beth's living room lights were burning as I pulled up the drive.

Before I reached the front stairs, Beth was on the porch in a flannel robe, silhouetted against the rectangle of light from the living room. Stapler scampered down the steps to greet me.

Beth shut the door behind us. She held me tight, her head on my chest, for a long time.

"So what did the police say?" I asked, my chin on her head.

She loosened her arms, lifted her face into mine. "I went out to the barn with them. Whoever it was had piled some rags and scraps of wood in a corner and threw gasoline on it. He pretty well spilled gasoline all over. He left behind a black duffel bag in there; he must have used it to carry all the stuff in. I guess I surprised him just as he was about to set everything on fire."

I wanted to tell her I was sorry, that I probably got her into this. Akibu knew getting to Beth was the perfect way to get to me. But I didn't say anything more, and after a while she tilted her head back again, smiled and said, "There's a bottle of Stolichnaya waiting for you on the kitchen table. Would you like a drink?"

"If you're having one."

"You bet I'm having one."

While she made the drinks, I went out to the back with a flashlight and looked for blood, pretty sure she never touched the guy. Had he been farther away, even if she'd aimed over his head, the widening shot cone might have caught him in the head. But if that happened, he wouldn't likely be getting up again. No doubt he got scared and tripped. Though I found no blood, I wouldn't have been surprised to find a loose bowel movement.

When I came into the kitchen I said, "Beth, I'm glad you had the coach gun. You did the right thing."

Her back was to me, mixing an old fashioned for herself and a Stoli on the rocks for me. "I don't know, Mike," she said without turning around. "I'm not sure I want to keep that thing around." Then she turned to me, a drink in each hand. "I don't think I have it in me to shoot someone."

We sat on the living room couch. I left plenty of room between us, but after a minute she scooted closer and, holding her drink in two hands, laid her head against my shoulder. We sat wordlessly for a long time, and then she opened one button on my shirt, slipped a hand in, made slow circles in the hair on my chest. I turned to look at her, and she lifted her face to mine. We kissed slowly, and then she leaned to set her drink down, her robe falling open. She had on a flannel nightgown underneath, and I cupped a hand under her breast. She gripped my fingers, moving my hand away, I thought in protest. Then she stood. "Come on," she said, and led me to her bedroom.

Beth's doorbell jangled at ten after nine the next morning, and woke us both. I bolted out of bed.

202

"It's okay, I'll get it," she said, slipping into her robe.

"Wait, I'll go with you." I sat on the edge of the bed a moment, rubbing my face.

"No, stay," she said. I felt like Stapler. I crawled back under the covers.

She came back a minute later. "It's someone from the County Fire Marshal's office. I sent him around to the barn." She sat on the side of the bed, her face hovering close to mine, and stroked my hair. "Sorry, I've got to get dressed." She kissed me, and I reached for her, but she pulled away. "Mike, the guy's waiting outside." She went into the bathroom and closed the door.

Half an hour later I was sitting in the living room when Beth brought the man through the front door: short, bald, wearing a rumpled trench coat and clutching a clipboard. He extended a hand. "Fire Marshal Dooney, McHenry County Fire Department," he said. "And you are?"

"Mike Duncavan," I said, knowing he wanted to know more.

He stared. "The, ah, man of the house?"

I nodded toward Beth. "She's the man of the house." Beth didn't laugh.

"Okay, then," he said to Beth. "Any ideas who might have done this?"

"No, no idea." Her eyes flicked to mine, and Fire Marshal Dooney picked up on that.

He looked at me. "No idea?" he said.

"No," I said. Then I looked at Beth. "But we should mention that guy at the art fair."

The Fire Marshal's eyes were on Beth.

"You tell him, Mike." He looked at me.

"It may not mean anything, but Beth was displaying her

artwork out front during the fair, and this strange-looking guy was hanging around for awhile. He asked if he could see the barn. Beth started to show him around, but she couldn't leave her tables."

He scribbled on his clipboard. "You have no idea who he was?"

"No, none."

"What did he look like?"

"Five-ten, twenty-five to thirty, skinny, long black hair. Had a tattoo here." I pointed to the inside of a forearm. "A dagger through a heart."

"And you don't have any idea who he was?" he asked again, jotting down the description.

"No."

When he finished writing, he lowered his clipboard, shifted his gaze from me to Beth to me again, trying to decide if we were believable. "Well, whoever did it was a rank amateur, lucky for you. I don't know what the motive was . . ." He did that thing with his eyes again. "But he had no idea what he was doing. By the way, what insurance company are you with?"

Beth told him.

"I was just about to make some coffee," I said. "Would you like some?"

"No, thanks," he said. "How much insurance do you carry?" He was looking at me.

"You'll have to ask the man of the house," I said, and walked into the kitchen.

After he left, Beth came into the kitchen. "He asked a lot of questions about you," she said.

"No problem," I said. "Look, you understand why I didn't want to get into anything about David Akibu. Maybe it's a little late, but I'd still like to keep you out of that."

She smiled, put a couple of glasses in the sink, started the water running. "Don't worry. It's too bizarre a story, anyway."

She was wearing a gingham shirt and snug Levis that emphasized her narrow waist, the curve of her hips. I slipped my arms around her. She turned, her back to the sink, put a hand on my chest, gently pushed me away.

"Mike," she said and cast her eyes down. She shook her head slowly.

I stood there not moving, unable to think of a word to say.

"Last night was wonderful, Mike, but nothing has changed, has it?" Her eyes penetrated mine.

"You still feel we're married in the eyes of the Lord?" I asked. I shouldn't have. I just couldn't think of anything else.

Her quick laugh was tinged with sarcasm. "Why do you ask?"

I shrugged.

"Is that your answer?" Her expression was hard, but then her shoulders relaxed and, leaning back against the sink, she hugged herself and turned her eyes to the floor. "I'm sorry, Mike." She shook her head again. "Jesus, you're my knight in shining armor, you really are." Then she looked at me. "But life isn't a fairy tale, is it?"

"So, then. Do we have a future?"

Her lips moved to a half smile and she gave her head that same slow shake. "You tell me, Mike. The answer to your question—the earlier one, about being married in the eyes of God? Yes. That's how I feel today. I can't tell you about tomorrow. I have a life. And you have no right to think you have some claim on me."

"Beth, Christ! I never thought for a minute I had a claim on you."

"So what's the answer then?"

I took my eyes off hers. "I'm sorry, what was the question?"

She was smiling up at me, her lips compressed. She laughed, a puff of air through her nostrils, patted my cheek, then slipping away into the living room she said, "Thanks for coming, Mike."

Shortly afterward we were at the front door.

"Listen, you be careful," I said. "You see anything suspicious, call the police right away."

"When I said thanks for coming, I really meant it, Mike," she said. "Thank you, for real." She pecked me on the lips, then opened the door.

"You're sure you don't want me to stay?"

"I'll be fine," she said, holding the door open for Stapler and me.

CHAPTER THIRTY-THREE

It was Saturday, a magnificent fall day in the country, and enroute home I turned into a wooded drive in the forest preserve, followed it to a grassy field with picnic tables and pulled into the parking area. No one else was around, so I let Stapler off his leash, sat at one of the tables and watched him sniff at inscrutable mysteries in the grass.

It made me wonder about what animals really do know. Stapler could see things with his nose better than I could see them with my eyes. He could see the image of things even after they were gone. He could see things in the dark, sense things a man could not realize in a million years. The human race, I thought, should show more respect. There were ways in which our dogs are distinctly superior.

Stapler was chewing on long blades of grass at the edge of the woods. A red Jeep Wrangler drove in and parked. Technically you weren't supposed to let dogs go unleashed in the forest preserve, so I got up to go over and get him, but when no one got out of the Wrangler, I sat down again. I saw the driver pick up a book and start reading.

My thoughts turned to the implications of the night before, and of this morning. Night and the morning, dark and light, yin and yang. I still could not believe I'd slept with Beth. I did not go to her house with that expectation. I did not go there even *wanting* that—I would never in a million years have thought it was a possibility. I still felt the afterglow of her body, the excitement of her touch.

But the weight of "what now?" descended darkly. I

wanted her more than anything a thousand good lifetimes could offer, and it occurred to me now that the clarity of vision that comes with age is not always a blessing—there are times you'd prefer the tinted glasses, the soft focus lens. Age may weaken the eyes but it sharpens the ability to see through bullshit—especially your own bullshit. Rationalization becomes harder. Ten years ago I would have been positive, at a moment like this, that I was finally ready for a lifetime with Beth if—please, God—she'd have me. But now I saw myself in the glare of a spotlight. I wasn't sure, even now, that I was ready.

The light faded slightly as a cloud drifted past the sun, and I looked up at an armada of lead-bottomed cumulus wandering across the sky, the kind you see on cool, sunny days, and suddenly I felt like I was standing atop a major watershed, looking down on the quiltwork of my life on one side, and as sure as rivers flow downhill, so was I going to, and I knew I had to decide, soon, which watershed I would follow. One way or another, like it or not, I was going.

When had I ever really taken charge of my life? I had lost everything I ever valued—except my honor, I liked to tell myself, and even that might be a neat little self-deception. Cheating on Beth, dipping my wick into another man's wife—a man who trusted me—those were not exactly badges of honor.

But now, if there was a chance, a small chance, that Beth would have me back, it was time to *be ready, to make myself ready*. With the thought of it, my heart started beating faster, my thoughts raced; I would call her, ask her to put me on probation. She would keep on living in Sutler's Grove; I would keep my apartment. And I would promise to remain celibate for as long as—whatever she says, she can name the time. And while I'm demonstrating my fidelity, we think about coming back together.

I wanted to call her right now on my cell phone, quickly decided against it. I would rehearse my plea.

I looked around for Stapler then. He was nowhere in sight. The Wrangler was gone too, and worry pulled at the edges of my mind. A blue van, which I had not noticed before, was parked near where the Wrangler had been.

"Stapler," I called. "Here, boy!" There was only silence. From where I sat, the van looked empty; but no one else was around. I scanned the woods that bordered the grassy field, straining for a glimpse of Stapler among the trees. I called to him again. No sight of him.

There was a cinder path leading into the woods and I started down it, the air cooler under the arching trees. I walked about fifty yards, came to a narrow dirt trail leading off to the right and took it, calling for Stapler, trying to keep anxiety from my voice. The trail was curving back toward the field, and when I saw open sunlight ahead, I squatted down for a view beneath the tree level. "Stapler!"

I turned to head back, now, my gut churning as the image of the blue van in the parking lot melted into the image of the blue van I shot at in the alley that night. I quickened my pace, wanting to run, but my bad ankle was throbbing like a toothache. Then I spotted a man running on the cinder path ahead, flashing into view as he crossed a break in the trees. He went out of sight, and when he came into view again, a rope of greasy black hair swinging rhythmically across his shoulders, I saw that it was the hippie from the art fair. I dashed to intercept him, a chisel of pain biting my ankle, and reached the main path just as he passed. He didn't see me. With one great heave of will I sprinted the few steps it took to overtake him and hit him high, and as he plunged to the cinders he let out an animal yelp; and I was on his back in an instant, swung an arm around his neck and jerked his head back. "Where's my dog?" I yelled.

"Help!" he screamed, then more desperately, *"Help!"*

With the benefit of a closer look, I now realized I'd never seen this guy before.

I was rolling off him, and in the same instant Stapler was next to me, dancing with quick, high-pitched barks. He started mock-growling, then, wanting to get in on the fun.

The pain in my ankle slowed my getting up, and the guy was on his feet before me. His knees were scraped and bleeding, his eyes wild. He backed away from me. "You're fucking crazy!"

I hobbled toward him, extended a hand. "Look, I'm really sorry, let me—"

"Stay the fuck *away from me!*" he yelled. He spun and ran away, and I watched him go until he reached the blue van. I slipped fingers under Stapler's collar and limped back. Before I got to my car, the van had roared out of the parking lot.

I took I-90 heading into the city, and reached the Kennedy wondering why things like that never seemed to happen to other people. Why couldn't I live like a dignified lawyer, attend the Society of Trial Lawyers' dinners and hobnob with people who never seem to roll in the dirt? I used to be terrific in front of a jury—what was I missing?

I punched a pre-set button on the radio and brought in WBEZ. Gretchen Helfrich was in the middle of an interview, her guest a doctor of some kind.

"I know you're pretty well known in your field, Doctor Wexler. Your specialty is what, oncology?"

"No, I'm a board-certified dermatologist, but my research is in skin cancers."

"So I guess you wouldn't call this junk science," she said.

"Definitely not junk science, no. But . . ."

"You believe it?"

"I believe there's definitely something there."

"But is it science? I mean, how well accepted is it in the field of medicine?"

"That's what I wanted to point out. All our studies so far are anecdotal. Still, the evidence is strong that dogs do sense these things. I mean, I've reviewed case after case of dogs behaving this way, persistently sniffing at specific areas of their owners' skin, making pests of themselves. And the person turns out to have a melanoma. Or they are developing a melanoma."

"Is it just skin cancer the dogs detect?"

"Well, basal cell carcinomas. Yes, I mean, we haven't looked at other types of cancers."

"Why do you suppose it is, Doctor, that this is just coming to light now? People have owned dogs since the dawn of time."

"It's like a lot of things in medicine, no one's ever made the connection before. If you think about it, it's an easy connection to miss. I mean, dogs like to sniff, and sometimes they make pests of themselves."

"So if someone's dog starts sniffing any part of the body, they should be concerned they might have cancer?"

"Persistently is the key word. If the dog shows persistence in sniffing a specific part of the skin, especially if it's a mole or a wart, the person should see their doctor right away. I certainly would. Unless it was my crotch; then I wouldn't worry."

Gretchen laughed, and as she ended the interview, I shut off the radio and looked over at Stapler. He was sitting up on the front seat, watching the road.

And I sat there a little dumbfounded, with Akibu's words ringing in my head: *the hyena knows things about the cosmos you could never begin to understand.*

I got off the Kennedy at Armitage, and when I reached my apartment I fed Stapler, then called my office to retrieve my answering machine messages. There was one from Mildred Temple, leaving her number in a worried voice and asking me to please call. It took a few seconds to remember who she was: the mother of Clyde Temple, in whose basement David Akibu had stayed briefly.

I punched the numbers into the phone, and was glad that she answered instead of her husband.

"Oh, I'm so glad you called me," she said, in what seemed a mix of angst and relief. But then she seemed unsure of what she wanted to say.

Finally she asked, "Did you ever find that David?"

"No. Do you know where he is?"

"No, I don't, but . . . we're worried about Clyde, our son?" A small tremor ran through her words now. "I know you said you're donating your time to the Red Cross? Well, we'll pay you, if you can help us find Clyde."

"Your son is missing?"

"He never came home from San Francisco, and he never called. Stupid, we never got the name of the people he was staying with there. He was supposed to come home two weeks ago. He didn't know what date exactly, he said he'd call when he knew, but he never did."

"Did you call the police?"

"They're no help. At first they wouldn't do anything; they said he wasn't gone long enough to be missing. When he still didn't come home I called them back, and they took a report, but that's all. Can I make an appointment, and come down to see you at your office?"

"I'm going to be in your neighborhood this afternoon. How's three o'clock?"

She said it would be fine and I hung up. Kim Price was gone, and now Clyde. I didn't want to commit to taking on her missing son's case, but I did want to know why David Akibu's friends were disappearing.

CHAPTER THIRTY-FOUR

I decided to drop by Kim's apartment building on the way to Edgebrook, check one more time, and I took Western north, turned onto Grace. I drove past the building, looking for a parking space, and spotted a "For Rent" sign in Kim's window. I parked in the next block and walked back.

I told the landlady over the intercom that I was inquiring about the vacant apartment.

When she came down and saw me through the glass of the vestibule door, she bunched her eyebrows and asked, "You're not really here about the apartment, are you?"

I shrugged. "Did Kim skip out on her rent?"

"Yeah." She drew back the corners of her mouth, annoyed. "And if you see her, you can tell her I gave away all of her furniture to the Salvation Army."

"Can I see the apartment?"

"What for?"

"I'm interested in an apartment in the neighborhood."

"Sure you are."

"I am," I said.

Her eyes moved away, thinking a minute. "No, you're not. I don't believe you for a minute, but I guess it can't hurt," she said. "Follow me."

The hardwood floors of Kim's apartment, the clean right angles of bare rooms rang with emptiness. "Looks like you just painted the place," I said.

"Kim painted before she moved in. I gave her a break on the first month's rent to do that."

"She was here, what, two months?"

"Yeah, well I don't even know when she left. Last couple of weeks I'd hear her coming and going in the middle of the night. Then, when her rent was two weeks overdue, I left a note under her door. But I never saw her again."

"Was anyone staying with her?"

"No, she lived alone. Look, just knock on my door when you're finished, okay?"

When she left, I went through the whole place, every room empty, clean-swept, even the closets—I couldn't even find dust on the shelves. In the bathroom the medicine chest was empty, too. Then I noticed a smudge in the glossy paint above the toilet, about shoulder height. The kind of mark left by a guy leaning sleepily on the wall in the middle of the night while taking a leak. I was pretty sure Kim Price didn't leave it there.

On the way out, I knocked on the landlord's door. "When was the last time you heard anyone in the apartment?" I asked.

She shrugged. "Not since I put the note under the door, but I don't remember exactly."

"Did you ever see anyone else besides Kim going into the apartment?"

"No. I'm sure Kim had friends, but I never paid any attention."

"Did you ever notice a blue Dodge van parked anywhere nearby?"

"Why are you asking all these questions?"

"I'm trying to find Kim."

She kept her eyes level for several seconds, then looked away. She massaged the back of her neck. "A beat-up old thing, with the back windows broke out?"

"That's it," I said.

"You couldn't help but notice, it was a little unsightly. I know it didn't belong to any of my tenants. I only saw it there at night."

"How often?"

"Fairly often. But I haven't seen it lately."

To get to Mrs. Temple's residence in Edgebrook, I took Addison over to Central. Big mistake. The Cubs game was just getting over, and traffic oozed along Addison with the speed of molten lava. At least it gave me time to think about Kim. She was almost certainly dead. I was sure Akibu had been staying in that apartment, probably sneaking in late at night. I should have staked the place out, planted my ass there for as long as it took. If I had done that, I'd have connected with Akibu for sure. Let's hear it for master detective work.

Mrs. Temple must have been watching for my arrival. I was just turning into her walk when she swung open the screen door.

"You must be a very good man," she said, ushering me into the living room. "Donating your time to the Red Cross like that, then coming to see us at a moment's notice." I sat in a comfortable chair; she sat on the couch, holding what looked like a framed picture face-down in her lap.

"Tell me about your son," I said.

"Hard to know where to begin. You could say Clyde is one of those kids who march to a different drummer. He dropped out of college. He keeps trying to find himself."

"Does he have a job?"

"No. Well, he's had several; he was a clerk at Walgreen's, and he delivered pizzas for awhile. I mean, those were summer jobs. He finished out the spring semester at SIU; then, when the summer was over, he decided not to go back. He went to visit a friend of his in San Francisco, someone he knew from college, who dropped out too. Clyde was only supposed to be gone two weeks."

"You said you don't know his friend's name?"

She lowered her chin as if to hide the color coming into her face, and shook her head. "I know it sounds stupid, but . . ."

I heard someone moving around in the kitchen, assumed it was her husband. I hoped he would stay there. "What about friends in the neighborhood?" I asked. "Can you give me any names?"

Her face colored again. "Clyde's like . . ." Her eyes went to the ceiling, she turned the picture over and clutched it to her bosom, then rocked back and forth. "He doesn't have many friends, I'm afraid." She brushed a knuckle at the corner of one eye, too late to catch a tear that slipped down her cheek. "I'm sorry," she said, and began to sob.

"Take your time," I said. "When you feel like it, I'd like to get a look at his room, if that's okay."

She bobbed her head and sniffled.

Then suddenly her husband was there, standing in the archway. "No, it's not okay," he said. For a guy in his sixties, he still looked like he could do you some damage. "What the hell are you doing here?"

"I called him, Ted. Please don't, Ted."

"Who are you working for?"

"Ted, I called him."

"No, who are you working for? You sure as shit ain't working for no Red Cross."

"Like the lady says, she called me. Now if you've got a problem with that, I'll just leave."

"Ted *please*, I told you, I called him. Don't you even care about Clyde?"

"You don't get it, Millie. Before this guy goes searching through our kid's stuff, I want to know who he's working for. Us or somebody else? Simple as that. You think these guys got some kind of a code of ethics?"

"Tell you what," I said. "I'll just come back another time when everybody's less edgy, okay?" I stood.

"Good idea," Ted said, and walked out of the room.

Mrs. Temple walked me to the door. "I'm so sorry. I'll talk to my husband; he's a good man, just a little—flinty sometimes." She opened the door, and as I was about to leave she said, "Oh, I almost forgot, here's Clyde's picture."

I looked at the long, dark hair, the skinny arms. Suspicion confirmed—it was the hippie, all right, Akibu's sidekick.

She didn't seem to notice; there was only supplication in her eyes. I wished I could have put her fears to rest, to tell her that I knew her son was alive. But I really didn't know that. He was alive when I saw him, a week ago. But by now, Akibu could have eaten his disciple's heart.

CHAPTER THIRTY-FIVE

First thing Monday morning I called Blake Canavan, asked him if he'd talked to the State's Attorney about broadening the investigation into Reggie Brockton's murder.

"I was going to call you this morning. I'm sorry, but he said exactly what I told you. It's up to the police, it's their decision."

"The police won't open an investigation on a cleared homicide," I said.

"What if you approached it from the aspect of the missing girl? That's an open investigation."

"I've already talked to the police about that. They're not interested in anything I told them."

"Mike, I did what I could. I was just on my way to court when you called. I got to go."

I carried the coffee pot down to the men's room to get fresh water, and when I came back, the light on the answering machine was glowing. I hit the play button. It was Phoebe Toplin, the beautician who'd worked with Kim Price. She'd left her home number, asked me to call her. Her tone was friendly, no sense of urgency. I started the coffee and dialed her number.

"You remember me?" she asked in a flirtatious drawl.

"How could I forget you?" I asked, feeling a little moronic.

"I think I might have some information for you, about Kim Price."

"Hang on," I said, my hands scrambling madly through

the papers on my desk in search of a pen. Snatching one, I said, "Okay, go ahead."

"Would you like to meet me somewhere?"

I didn't want to meet her anywhere, I wanted the information, wanted it now. But lady luck had not been favoring me lately—what if I scared her off? "Sure," I said. "When?"

"I suppose a good lookin' fella like yourself probably's got a date tonight?"

"Nope, no plans. Just staying home with my dog. A lonely prospect," I added, for the sake of clarity.

"Tell me about it." She lived on the north side, near Lawrence Avenue. I arranged to meet her at the Green Mill at eight.

I found her sitting in a booth near the back, holding a long-neck Old Style on the table like a scepter. I slid in across from her, ordered a double Stoli on the rocks. "I was glad you called, I've been worried about Kim," I said. "Do you know where I can find her?"

She put the long-neck to her lips, tipped it back. She put it down. "Maybe. So tell me about yourself," she said.

I shrugged, wondering what kind of game we were supposed to be playing. "Nothing much to tell."

She waited for me to say more. When I didn't, she said, "This whole private detective thing, it sounds really exciting." She took another pull on her beer and smiled. "How does a guy get started in something like that?"

"Long story," I said.

"I got time. Is it like on TV?"

"Nothing like TV."

"You carry a gun?"

"Sometimes, when I'm on an investigation and think I might need it. But tell me about you, Phoebe."

"Is being a private eye like in the mystery books?"

"No. It's pretty boring, actually."

"I'm a reader." She nodded once for emphasis, then smiled sweetly. "I read a lot of mystery books. Do you know I got the highest G.E.D. score ever recorded in the State of Tennessee?"

"Wow," I said. "I didn't know they kept statistics on things like that."

"They do." She leaned on her chubby arms. "Mysteries, they're my favorite books. Romances, too."

"Do you know Kim well?" I asked, hoping I hadn't shifted from the literary plane too abruptly.

"No. Well, kinda. I only met her when she started at Magic Moments, but we seemed to hit it off. You ever been married?"

"Twice," I said.

"Three times for me. All of 'em lowlifes, too."

"I'll bet it's soured you on men," I said.

"You kidding? I love men." She gave my arm an affectionate squeeze. "So. Do you think I'm pretty?" She massaged the back of my hand.

It took me by surprise. When I didn't answer right away, she pulled her hand back, put it in her lap. "Maybe I shouldn't have called you," she said. "I get the feeling maybe you don't like being here with me." She lifted her purse, klunked it onto the table.

I put a hand on hers, patted it. "Phoebe," I said, looking deep into her eyes. "Phoebe." Her expression softened a little. "I guess it won't hurt to tell you—first time I walked into that beauty shop, I couldn't keep my eyes off you. But you had to notice."

She tipped the long-neck to her lips, drained it, and said, "You've got more bullshit than Badger Breeders." I was afraid she was going to leave, but then she said, "I started a tab." She looked around for the waitress.

I definitely needed more Stoli. I knocked my glass back and ordered another round and tried to shift my internal gearbox into patient mode. This lady could be holding the key to the entire case, and I had the feeling that she might bolt like a deer at any minute.

"Tell me about yourself," I said. "Lived in Chicago long?"

She belched and shook her head. "Uh-uh. After I divorced the last lowlife, I came up here for college, to better myself, and I just wound up staying. Did you know I graduated first in my class from cosmetology college? They said I could've got a job anywhere I wanted. I sure wasn't going back home."

She told me about growing up in rural Tennessee, about her marriages, about her daddy who'd worked in the lumberyard all his life.

"Did you know my daddy invented Krispy Kreme doughnuts?" she said.

"No," I said, with as much astonishment as I could muster.

She bunched her lower lip and bobbed her head. "Yep. For a while, Daddy had a route with Snap-On tools, and he started selling his doughnuts out of the truck. This one guy, customer of his, tricked him into giving him the recipe, then went and got himself a patent," she said. "And the rest is history."

She droned on, one hard luck story followed by another bad break, each tale a sad country song waiting to be written. I numbed my brain with vodka, lots of it, hoping that sooner or later we'd get around to Kim Price.

Then, after nearly two hours, I began to see her truly, this fellow voyager on the storm-tossed sea of life. And she really wasn't that bad-looking, either.

Still later, as I washed my hands in the men's room, my mirror image swaying like a redwood about to fall, I told myself I had to get down to business. But first I had to find out about Kim Price.

When I returned to the table and saw her smiling up at me, I had an odd feeling that we'd been lovers in a former life. Then, captivated by that angelic face, I noticed for the first time she had a pair of breasts you could bury your face in and want to die there.

"Watch my purse, will you, Hon?" she said. "I got to pee."

I watched her make her way to the back, waited for the door of the ladies' room to close behind her, then snatched up the purse, rifled through it, and found what I was hoping for: an address book. I flipped to the P's and—thank you, Jesus!—there it was, *Kim Price.*

The address and number on Grace Street had been crossed off. Another phone number, no address, was penciled above it, an area code I didn't recognize. I ripped out the page, stuffed it in my shirt pocket, crammed the address book into the purse and dropped it back onto the seat.

When she returned, she didn't sit down. "You gonna take me home, Hon?"

"Phoebe, I sure want to, but I got a duty to my client. I can't leave until you tell me about Kim Price."

She rolled her eyes to the ceiling. "O-kay," she said in what I hoped was only mock exasperation. Slipping back into the booth, she said, "Honestly, you private eyes and your clients."

"Phoebe, just tell me how can I get in touch with Kim, that's all I need."

"I can't tell you that."

"Why not?"

" 'Cause I promised not to."

"You promised Kim?"

She shook her head. "I promised not to say anything."

"Promised who?"

She shook her head.

"She's alive?"

"A course she's alive," she huffed. "Why shouldn't she be alive?"

"Are you sure? When did you last talk to her?"

"Day before yesterday."

"Did she tell you she's in some sort of trouble?"

She reached across the table, pinched my cheek. "Take me home, Hon."

She lived in a third-floor walkup, a courtyard building on Brentwood. In the living room she put Patsy Cline on the CD player, and asked me if I wanted a drink. "Sure," I said.

"Vodka?"

"On the rocks, please," I said, still standing.

She started for the kitchen, then turned back to me, pinched my cheek again, giving it a shake this time. "You know how cute you are?"

I didn't know the right answer, so I just stood there with a stupid grin, and then she snaked her hand to the back of my head, pulled my face down and started kissing me slowly on the mouth.

Next thing I knew, she was undoing my trousers, pushing me toward the couch. I shuffled backward as my trousers slipped to my knees, at the same trying to unbutton her blouse, and then I fell onto the couch and she undid her own buttons, dropped the blouse on the floor and then whipped off her bra somehow, setting loose those wonderfully ample orbs.

She leaned over me. "You like these?" she whispered. She squeezed her breasts together, pink nipples inching toward my face, staring at me goggle-eyed like an albino monkey. Before I could answer she pulled my face into them, and then I was sure I was going to suffocate.

Now she was on her feet, pulling at her slacks, hopping on one foot, which caused a lamp to gyrate on a table, then finally ripped them off. "You do have protection, don't you?" she puffed, wearing nothing but a pair of capacious yellow panties.

I blinked, pretended I didn't understand, and reached for her.

She took a step backward. "You do have a condom, don't you?"

I shook my head. "Sorry."

Her forehead bunched. "How could you come out to see Phoebe and not bring protection?"

I turned up my palms, then pointed at my crotch. "You know, you could just maybe . . ."

The backs of her hands went to the sides of her yellow panties. "That's great for you," she said, "but what about Phoebe?" Snatching her blouse and her bra and her slacks from the floor, she said, "I'm sorry, but you're gonna have to leave."

She walked toward the back of the apartment, buttocks like a pair of bowling balls alternately rising and falling, and disappeared. I sat there several minutes, and when I heard no more sound, I let myself out.

The following morning I got out of bed in slow increments, my pulse banging in my ears, a couple of sharp stones pressing the back of my eyeballs. I found my shirt lying on the floor and, hoping I was remembering with some accuracy the night before, checked the pocket. It was there, the page with Kim Price's phone number.

I flopped back on the bed, an arm shielding my eyes from the light which somehow caused those stones in my head to vibrate, and with my stomach sinking lower, I thought of Beth. My firm resolution to be ever faithful had been when? Two days ago?

I pulled on a bathrobe, let Stapler out in the yard and called directory assistance. The area code was a small town near Greenville, Mississippi. I dialed the number, let it ring fifteen times.

I took a shower.

CHAPTER THIRTY-SIX

I headed down to the Loop in a driving rainstorm, my spirits lower than the torrents rushing through the sewers, and when I reached the office the red light on the answering machine was blinking. There were two messages, both from Phoebe Toplin. "Morning, Sweety, call me, okay?" The second one said, "Did you oversleep, you naughty boy?"

I made a pot of coffee and tried Kim's number again. This time a woman answered.

"Kim?" I said, pretty sure it was her, then by the silence that followed I knew it was.

"Who is this?" Kim, all right, a trace of fear rippling the edges of her voice.

"Mike Duncavan, Kim," I said. "I've got to talk to you."

"No one's supposed to know where I am—how did you get this number?"

"You're running from David Akibu. Why?"

Another five seconds passed. Then angrily, "Who gave it to you?"

"Kim, please, talk to me."

"Was it Phoebe?"

"I need to talk to you, it's important."

"It had to be her; she was the only one had it. Fucking, cracker, *bitch!*"

"Phoebe didn't give me your number. Look, your secret's safe with me, just answer a few questions."

"Yes she did, I know she did, no one else had it."

"Kim, listen, five minutes, that's all . . ."

"I don't want to talk to you. Please, please, just leave me alone."

"Tell me what you know about David Akibu."

"Please, I've got to go. Goodbye."

"Kim, don't hang up. You called me that night, remember? You needed to talk to me? You said he was evil?"

"Goodbye."

"No, listen. You're in this, Kim, like it or not. A little girl could die. An innocent man could . . ."

"*I* could die," she interrupted, her voice breaking.

"You don't have to live this way. Help me get him, then you can live your own life in peace."

"Please, stop," she said. "You don't know what you're up against. He has powers; he'll kill you. He'll kill me, too. I'm going to say goodbye now."

"No. If you hang up, I'm coming down there. I'll find you."

"No, you won't. I'll move somewhere else. Can't you understand? I just want to live."

"Kim, just tell me where can I find him, that's all."

"No. Stop bothering me. I will never, never talk to you."

"Then talk to the police. They'll protect you."

She was weeping now. "I'm begging you, please—forget that I'm alive." The line clicked dead. I started to redial, then hung up. She was scared senseless. She'd never cooperate.

I sat back, my mind swimming in the doldrums of this case, of my life. Kim was alive, at least. Which meant I couldn't pin her disappearance on Akibu. Well, her disappearance, yeah, but not her death. I felt like a starving man chewing on a steel pipe.

If Kim would just talk, it was all over, I was sure of it. Justin would go free; Akibu would be put away. But there was no way I could make her talk to me. At that moment, with my jaw clenched so tight I thought I might break a tooth, I wanted to kill Kim Price myself.

The phone rang. I reached for it, my hand hovering at the halfway point, and waited for the answering machine to come on. "It's Phoebe. You gonna call me, Honey?"

I sipped the dregs of my coffee and stared out the window at the parade of umbrellas below, her voice bringing back the night-before-follies, and when I turned around and saw Beth's picture smiling back from the credenza, I went over and turned it around.

That last conversation with Beth, as we stood at her front door on Saturday morning, hung on my mind like a cobweb. She'd asked me what was the answer, but I didn't know the question. *Yeah, you did. Mike, the master of self-deception. You asked her if she thought you had a future together. She said, You tell me.* Was it up to me, alone? Then, what would my answer be? The answer was last night. Only want of a condom kept me from plunging my willie into one more bimbo.

But I had not actually had sex. And fellatio, which in my pitiful state I tried to settle for, wasn't really sex, by decree of the President of the United States. The truth lay in the words of an earlier Democrat: I had lusted in my heart. And then some. I wanted my wife back, and I couldn't resist bimbos. I was pathetic.

Thoughts of my for-want-of-a-condom defeat the night before brought to mind a book, *The Myth of Heterosexual AIDS*, the controversial thesis of which held that unless you or your partner were in one of the high risk groups—an intravenous drug user, say, or a homosexual—your chances of contracting HIV were minuscule. For some reason I never quite followed, the book had enraged the gay community. I wondered where Justin stood on that.

And then it hit me so hard my head reeled like I was back in the ring. Justin! I needed to talk to him, and needed to do it now.

I managed to get into the jail that afternoon, prepared to ask some hard questions, but when I saw Justin shuffling toward me I was alarmed by how thin he'd become, and I mellowed a little. He looked so frail. His orange jumpsuit hung on him like a shroud.

To my surprise, he spoke first. "Do you think there's any hope, Mike? Of ever getting out of this place?" His eyes, set back in the hollows of his face, cut sideways, as though pondering the answer to his own question, and then his hand fluttered to his forehead, its skin drum-tight, and brushed back a wisp of hair.

I ignored the question. "You lied to me, Justin."

His head jerked up, eyes searching mine as if I'd slapped him. "What do you mean?"

"I mean you lied to me about David Akibu."

"What are you talking about?" He held my gaze as if trying to get a look behind my eyes. Then his eyes shifted a little, as though he were deciding something. He shook his head, looked down at his hands.

I waited, felt the blood beginning to boil up my neck.

"Look at me," I said. He kept his eyes averted. My temples grew hot. "Listen, you little butt-fucker, you lied to the police about being in that building, and now you think you can make a jackass out of me. If I could get my hands on you right now, I'd squeeze your throat until your eyeballs popped. You tell me, right now, what you know about David Akibu or I'm walking out of here and giving your mommy my final statement."

He still didn't look up. "I don't know how to say it."

"Then you just answer my questions, and you better give me straight answers this time or I'm outta here."

He nodded quickly but still didn't look at me.

"First off, how many times did you see David Akibu at that building?"

"Twice," he mumbled, looking at the backs of his hands.

"Have you seen him since?"

"No," he said emphatically, and his eyes met mine. "That's the honest-to-God truth."

"Truth, huh? You had a long conversation with him that first time, didn't you?"

He nodded, moving his eyes off mine again.

"And then the second time you had an even longer conversation."

He nodded once more.

"And you went into the building with him."

His lips moved, and he mumbled something. Somewhere a steel door slammed, and I couldn't hear his answer.

"Goddammit, speak up. You went into the building with him?"

"Yes!" It was the yelp of a kicked dog. The guard looked over. Justin squeezed his eyes shut and turned his face away.

"And you had sex with him in that building, didn't you?"

His chin bunched and his lower lip trembled and then his eyes squeezed out tears, which left tracks down both cheeks. He bobbed his head. "I betrayed Richard," he said. "He was home on his deathbed, and I promised I'd be faithful, and I betrayed him. God forgive me." He doubled over as though I'd punched him in the stomach. *God forgive me!*

God might, but at the moment I wasn't sure I would. "And you used a condom?"

He sniffled, wiped his eye with his shoulder. He didn't answer.

"Listen you little fuck, answer me! You used a condom?"

He looked at me with wide eyes, a plea for mercy. Then he pumped his head up and down.

"Now tell me, Justin, what did you do with the condom?"

At first he had no reaction. Then his brow tightened, his expression grew bewildered. "What are you . . . ?"

"Answer the fucking question. What happened to the condom?"

His eyes darted left and right. "Why, I left it there," he said.

Back in my office there were two more calls from Phoebe on the answering machine. I erased them and sat at my desk under a cloud of remorse that I seemed, at the moment, to share with Justin Ambertoe. My brother in that Fraternal Order of Unfaithful Bastards.

Then I called Stan Janda, told him everything about Justin's liaison with Akibu.

He seemed to mull it over. "Jesus Christ," he said. "Let me see if I got this straight. This Akibu guy lets Justin pork him just so he can collect his semen. Then he deposits it on the dead kid?"

"That's about it," I said. Below my office window a bus released its brakes, a sound like a harmonica.

"Ho-ly shit. This guy is diabolical," he said. I watched the bus edging into traffic. "I believe you, Mike," he said, as if my credibility was in need of shoring. "But we're not gonna sell this theory to anyone." A theory, he called it.

"I'm willing to bet my Omni that Akibu's still got the rubber," I said. "He may have already used it again, on the kid they haven't found."

"Be great to catch him with it."

"Right," I said. "We could always ask the prosecutor to get a warrant to search for a used condom at the premises of a non-suspect whose whereabouts are unknown. And it would be great to hit the Grand Slam in the lottery." I started to say goodbye.

"Mike, what about Canavan?"

"What about him?" I was pretty sure I knew where this was going.

"This puts a whole new light on everything, doesn't it? I'm thinking maybe we should approach him again, let him know what really happened."

I had a feeling he didn't mean "we."

"As I said before, you're the lawyer, Stan. But think about this. Justin stepped in it real good when he lied to the police the first time, telling them he'd never even been in that neighborhood before. Then he comes clean with a new story, the whole truth, nothing but. Do you want to admit to the prosecutor that your client's been caught in one more lie?"

"Well, let's think this through. If *you* told him, off the record, would that be an admission?"

"It wouldn't be. But why the hell would they believe any of it?"

"It's worth a try."

"Then you're the one who's going to have to call," I said, and then I said goodbye.

CHAPTER THIRTY-SEVEN

A couple of weeks passed, the passage of my life and my investigation both becalmed like twin ships on the Sargasso Sea, and then one afternoon out of nowhere a fresh wind began to blow.

I was sitting at my office window, watching the stream of pedestrian traffic, pondering a certain paradox of autumn: how the trees shed their leafy raiment in the fall, while the hoards of secretaries gliding below my window do something of the opposite. Gone are the low, scoop necks, the halter-tops of summer. The flesh is covered, the view denied. But at least the crisp air signaled the promise of December, which would bring women bundled in winter coats, snowflakes in their hair, tantalizing as Christmas packages waiting to be unwrapped. So, I happen to love women. Is that so wrong?

That's when the phone rang. "Legal Investigations, Mike Duncavan," I said absently, picturing a long-legged blonde with snowflakes in her hair, wearing nothing but a fur coat.

"Hey Mike, it's Nate Wilcox, remember me?" he said. The name didn't set off any bells, but the western drawl teased my memory. "Understand you was down to Texas talkin' with my buddy, Elmer."

That would be Elmer Bumpp. "Oh Nate, right!" I said, sitting up.

"I run into Elmer last week over to Meltrey. He said you was a good guy, told me about that business you're working on in Chicago."

"Yeah, Elmer was a big help," I said, wondering where this was going.

He paused. "He said he went ahead and told you about the, ah—hyena deal up there. I suppose there's no harm in him tellin' it. Way he talked, maybe some good could come out of it. He said something about you was trying to solve a murder of some kids?"

"That's right."

"How you coming with that?"

Now I was really wondering, but I said, "I wish it was coming better."

"Would it help if you had the license number? Of the truck?"

"Truck?"

"The blue van, the one that we loaded the hyena into."

"You mean you've got the license number?" I snatched up a pen.

"Yeah, I wrote it down on the back of a business card that night. When Elmer told me about you coming down to Texas, I looked in my wallet. I still got it, believe it or not. If you want it."

"Hell, yeah, I want it." He read off the number. I jotted it down on a Post-It.

"I just hope it helps," he said.

I wanted to crawl through the phone lines and kiss him on both cheeks. Hell, on the lips. I thanked him and, before he said goodbye, I took down his phone number. "I may need to call you back," I said.

I called Marty Richter, who had shifted to the afternoon watch. "Can you run a plate for me?" I gave him the number.

"I'll call you back," he said, and when he hung up I

hoped he meant soon, and I stared at the phone until it rang again, ten minutes later.

"Your plate checks to a '95 Dodge Ram. Black Rhino Imports, Inc., 415 N. Seeley, Chicago. This wouldn't be one with a few holes in it, by any chance?"

"I hope so."

"I'd think you'd want to stay far away from that one," he said.

"Marty, I think I just got a big break."

"Listen, Mike—" His voice trailed off.

"What?"

"You plan to go poking around over there?"

"What do you think?"

"Be careful. And call me when you get home."

I called the Secretary of State's Office, Corporations Division, to get information on the company's officers and the registered agent, and listened to my own pulse beating in my ears as I waited on hold. Akibu, I thought, was nearly in my sights.

But then the guy came back on. "You did say Black Rhino Imports? We have no listing of a corporation by that name."

My spirits sank. "How are you spelling it?"

"I tried every way I could think of. There's no listing."

That should have been no surprise, I thought as I hung up. I walked down to the County Building to check the Assumed Name Index. It was a long shot, but in theory any person who operates a business with a name other than his own is required to register the name and ownership with the index. But the law had no teeth, and a lot of people ignored it. No listing there, either.

Since it was rush hour I went home first, fed Stapler, ate

236

dinner, slipped the snub-nosed Python onto my belt and drove over to the west side address. It was nearly eight o'clock when I got there, an area of old factory buildings now mostly abandoned.

I had been assigned to this district right out of the police academy. Even then, the light manufacturing companies in the area had begun their migration to modern industrial parks in the suburbs, and many of the structures were vacant shells. The companies that stayed frequently suffered burglaries in the night, the calls coming in after sunrise from frustrated managers arriving for work. We'd search the building, the exposed brick walls and old machinery looking like movie sets for a Charles Dickens novel, and every so often we'd nab a burglar still inside.

The address I was looking for was at the end of a short block that dead-ended against a railroad embankment. I pulled around the corner and parked under a sodium vapor lamp. There were no other cars around, and no lights burned in any of the buildings that I could see. I walked down the middle of the street, the cracked sidewalks on either side choked with weeds and windblown newspapers, to the last building, supposedly the home of Black Rhino Imports. Above the door there was only a faded sign that said: *Felsenthal Fasteners.*

The structure was three stories high, with glass block windows on the first floor that permitted no view inside. At the end, near the railroad embankment, was a set of doors to the loading dock, their green paint flaking. I snapped on the flashlight, peered through the windows. It did not seem to have been used in a long time.

I crossed the street to take in the whole facade. The line of windows on the second floor, where the offices would have been, was plate glass, which had not been washed in decades. Nowhere was there a sign that said: Black Rhino Imports.

I drove home, feeling that I'd just driven my investigation into one more cul de sac.

The morning Justin Ambertoe's trial started, I did not attend. There was nothing I could do for him in that courtroom. There was nothing I could do for anyone in any courtroom. I was beginning to believe—a thought which crouched in my mind like a leopard in the grass—that there wasn't much I could do for Justin Ambertoe, period.

CHAPTER THIRTY-EIGHT

That afternoon, the rays of the low sun turned the factory's red brick facade to dying embers and pierced the second-floor windows, where the man who called himself David Akibu was taking medical instruments from a leather Gladstone bag and setting them out on a long table. A pair of black leather straps, nailed to the table's surface, lay unbuckled at the table's center, and smoke from burning incense uncoiled out of bowls at each end.

The bag emptied, Akibu carried an elongated object bundled in orange cloth to the table and unwrapped it, exposing a long knife, the sunlight flashing off its blade, igniting the gemstones encrusted in the hilt. He pressed the cold flat of the steel to his forehead and, eyes closed, stood a moment, mumbling words of a forgotten language. Then he carefully set the knife on the table.

He went into the corridor, to the door of the next room, and unlocked it. He crossed to the little girl, who was sitting handcuffed to a chair in the middle of the room. Lawanda Henry lifted her eyes to him, but did not speak. In the corner, the caged hyena launched himself to his feet and stared over, its ribs bulging like exposed lath.

"Tonight, little one," he said, stroking Lawanda Henry's hair. "Tonight, all of your grief, all of your earthly pain, will come to an end. After tonight, you will be a part of the ages."

Lawanda lowered her head and wept bitterly, but Akibu took no notice. He went over to the hyena, patted the top of its cage and, with a kindly smile, whispered a single word: "Tonight."

239

CHAPTER THIRTY-NINE

At the end of the second day of Ambertoe's trial, the attorneys had still not finished picking a jury, according to the evening news. The following morning, I pumped iron for about two hours. Then, instead of going to the office, I went grocery shopping, and after that I took Stapler to the vet for his rabies shots. Then I went back home and cleaned my apartment.

I don't know why I bothered going to the office at all. It was late afternoon when I left home, a dark October sky dumping cold rain on the world and snarling rush hour traffic, and when I reached the office the answering machine light showed I had a single message. I hit the play button.

"You son of a bitch!" said Phoebe Toplin. "You think you can just toss Phoebe aside after Phoebe let you see her naked?"

Not completely naked, I thought, which, in the wincing of my mind's eye, now seemed a small mercy.

I erased the message and sat at the window, the rain having slowed to a drizzle, and I watched the parade of vehicles approaching on Wells under the El tracks, their headlights illuminated, their opposite image reflected in the rain-glazed street. It was like looking into an equal-but-opposite nether world with the car's twin just under the surface, attached by the tires. For a moment, I thought there must really be such a place, a world where the hyena in the park lived in the hours of daylight. Maybe, if I could get down under there somehow, I'd find David Akibu.

The phone rang. "Mike Duncavan," I said absently. No one spoke. I sat up, straining to catch some sound, some background noise.

Then a woman's voice said, "I have some important information for you." I was pretty sure it was Kimberly Price.

"Okay," I said. "Who's calling?"

"Do you want the information or not?"

"Sure," I said, grabbing a pen, rummaging through the clutter on my desk for something to write on. "Don't you want to tell me who this is?"

"No," she said. Then, "Look, it's Kim Price. I'm really scared, okay? I think he's going to kill someone today."

"Who is?"

"Listen motherfucker, you know who!" Then, her voice breaking, she said, "Don't make this hard for me."

"Okay, okay, please don't hang up."

"I told you, anyway. That's all I know, I done my part."

"No, wait. Can you tell me where, when?"

"I don't know where!" She was crying now. "All I know is it's supposed to go down today."

"Is it the missing girl, Lawanda Henry?"

"I don't know for sure. I think so."

"You got this from who?"

"Goodbye." The line clicked dead.

I pulled open a drawer, found the page I'd torn from Phoebe Toplin's phone book, and dialed Kim's number, listened to it ring. Then: "We're sorry, but the number you dialed has been disconnected."

CHAPTER FORTY

It was after five o'clock, the height of rush hour, and still drizzling a little. I took a pistol from the bottom desk drawer, checked the magazine. It was the only gun I had in the office, a .32 Walther PPK, a gift from a grateful client who'd inherited it but had no interest in guns. A little underpowered for my taste—I found myself craving the heft of the .357 Magnum, but the Walther would have to do.

The magazine was full: eight rounds. In a filing cabinet I found a half-empty box of cartridges, took one, chambered a round, then dropped the magazine out and added another cartridge. Now the gun held nine; I wished it held a lot more. Then I picked up a small flashlight, and took a pair of Nikon compact binoculars from the windowsill and stuck them in my jacket pocket.

All I could think to do was drive over to that factory building. For all I knew, it could be over already. I walked as quickly as my bad ankle would allow to the La Salle Hotel Parking Garage, retrieved my car and turned into rush hour traffic. Inching along Washington Boulevard, I dismissed an idea to call the police. I had nothing to go on and, as far as the police were concerned, I was more a criminal than Akibu was—if they found out I shot at the fleeing vehicle. And this could also be a false alarm, though something in my gut said it wasn't. It felt more like show time for a one-night stand, and I didn't know the music.

The girl could already be dead. Or I could blow the whole deal, spook Akibu into going further underground.

Or I could come on him unexpectedly, when he was doing nothing wrong. I still had nothing on him, after all. Well, I had a lot on him, all personal, and if I caught up with him I could at least adjust his clock a little.

I turned south onto Halsted, beating a nervous tattoo on the steering wheel as I moved a foot or two at a time, and when I finally slid down the westbound ramp of the Eisenhower Expressway, I dialed Marty Richter's home number on my cell phone, not really sure what I wanted to say to him. But maybe he'd have some advice.

Donna answered. "He's in the den with a cocktail, Mike. I'll get him."

Marty picked it up, his tongue a little thickened by his martini. "What's going on?"

"The sun's below the yardarm?" I asked.

"Way below. You're in your car? Come on over."

In that moment I admitted to myself the real reason I'd called him: I wanted backup. "Just wondering if you might be in for a little adventure," I said. I explained about the anonymous call, told him where I was going.

When I finished, he said, "You mean you want me to come with you?"

"Well, yeah, that's the general idea."

He didn't say anything for a full five count. "Mike, Jesus. In the first place, this is police business."

"No, the police aren't interested."

"You know what I mean. If you've got what you think you've got, then it's a matter for the police, not you. Regardless of whether they're interested. In the second place, I'm half buzzed. And in the third place, I gave up chasing bad guys down alleys a long time ago. Now I conduct roll call. I sit in my office and approve case reports. I yell at patrol officers who shoot at moving vehicles. That's my life now, until I retire."

I was oozing along in stop-and-go traffic, and at that moment I looked up just in time to slam on the brakes, thus preventing another whiplash lawsuit. As I sat there with the engine idling, I suddenly felt ashamed, testing Marty's friendship this way. What the hell was wrong with me? I pictured Marty sipping a martini in his den with Donna, each of them happy in the other's company, which they took for granted. They took for granted their brick bungalow and neat lawn in a block of brick bungalows and neat lawns. Took for granted the photos of their children covering the living room walls. What Marty and I had in common was past, gone. The two of us were in very different places now, and suddenly I was drowning in a pool of envy. I had no kids, no home of my own, no wife and no future. What I had was an eighteen-year-old Dodge Omni in need of a muffler.

"Mike, are you there?" Marty asked.

"Yeah. Listen, Marty, this was really lame-brained, I'm sorry I bothered you. No kidding, enjoy your cocktails. Give Donna my love."

"Mike, come on over, I got a full bottle of Stoli waiting for you. Donna's standing here nodding her head. She wants you to come. Here," he said, handing the phone to Donna.

"Hey, Mike," she said, "we're just throwing on some steaks. There's a big one here with your name on it. Why don't you come on over?"

"I can't."

"Come on. You going to disappoint me?"

"Let's do it sometime soon." I said goodbye, and hung up.

CHAPTER FORTY-ONE

The rain had stopped by the time I turned onto Seeley. I parked at the corner and walked down to the dead-end, to the abandoned building that was supposed to house Black Rhino Imports. This time, a dim light flickered from the second floor windows of the old factory. I went to the loading dock doors, now bathed in the pale light from the street lamp across the street, and peeked through the glass. I didn't need a flashlight to see the blue van squatting there, back windows shot out, several holes in the sheet metal.

I tried the door next to the loading dock. Locked. Then I went around to the side along the tracks and made a complete circuit of the building, trying all the doors. Most of them had not been opened in decades. All of them were locked.

Returning to the front, I stood in the middle of the street and scanned the illuminated windows of the upper floor. For a second, I thought I saw a shadowy movement.

I crossed to the abandoned factory on the other side of the street, this one a two-story, looking for a way to the roof. Around the back, where the light from the street lamp did not reach, I snapped on my flashlight and found a rusty fire escape clinging to the side of the building, its spring-loaded lower section sagging with age. I jumped for it, and on the third try I caught hold of it and pulled it down.

I climbed to the roof and crossed to the street side and knelt behind the parapet. From here I could see almost directly into the second-floor windows across the way. There were two large rooms, both illuminated with candles. In the one on the right, which was more brightly lit, a long table was spread with some kind of metal objects. At first I thought the other room was empty, but as my eyes adjusted, I saw something—or thought I did—that shot fire through my knees.

A look through the binoculars confirmed it. There was a little girl in the room, sitting sideways on a straight-backed chair, her head leaning on an arm draped over the top. Her other arm was handcuffed to a chair leg.

Then as I watched, the shadowy figure of a man came through the doorway into the room. Moving in that ultra-silence which binoculars bestow, he picked up something from a box in the corner, and walked out again. The child seemed to pay him no attention. She may have been asleep.

Then the man reappeared in the next room, which was more brightly-lit. Dressed in flowing red robes, it had to be David Akibu. He put something down on the table, and I could see now that the table was set out with surgical instruments. Smoke rose up from incense bowls at either end of the table, and at its center lay one long, gleaming knife. I remembered the words of Dieter Braacht, which sent a thousand spiders crawling up my back: *They will cut out the child's liver, the kidneys, while she is still alive. The more she screams, the more powerful the medicine's going to be.*

I lowered the binoculars, my hands trembling a little, anxious to do something now. But what? Should I call the police? What could I tell them? The only thing was to get into the building, and get in fast.

Just then another car came around the corner, a dark, late model Buick, and pulled up behind mine. The lights blinked off, the driver got out and stood looking around, a heavyset white guy in a fedora. Then he walked to my car, looked in the window.

He started across the street, but halfway across he stopped, turned to look at my car again. I raised the binoculars. Now he was walking toward the abandoned factory, taking his time. It was Marty Richter.

I swung the binoculars back to the room on the left. The little girl hadn't moved.

I ran to the fire escape, down the rusty steps, around the building and crossed the street to Marty, who was peering through the loading dock windows when I reached him.

He turned to me and, without saying hello, wagged his head toward the bullet-riddled van. "That your handiwork?"

"Marty, I've got to get in there, and right now," I said. I briefed him on what I saw.

"Are you sure the kid was handcuffed?"

"No, I'm not," I said. "I got to go."

"Okay, listen, I'll call for a beat car to meet us. God only knows what I'll tell the dispatcher."

"No time, Marty," I said. I went to the wooden door next to the loading dock and smashed my good foot into it, at the point where the lock meets the jamb. Nothing happened. I tried it once, twice, three times. On the fourth try, splinters flew and the door swung open. I bolted up the stairs, knowing that the element of surprise was gone now. Marty was chugging up behind me.

The second-floor hallway door was propped open with a doorstop. I drew the Walther and, with my shoulder to the inside of the jamb, peeked around the corner.

A corridor painted in industrial green enamel ran the length of the building, with rows of doors on either side. Two doors stood partially open, the doors to the two rooms in which the candles were burning. I started into the corridor, moving slowly, and now Marty was behind me. "You

247

take the first room," he said, and brushed past me to the next doorway. I squatted just outside the first door, saw Marty stop at the second one and peek around the edge.

I did the same. The little girl was alone, sitting on the far side in the dim candlelight, thirty feet away, handcuffed to the chair. When she saw me her mouth opened and her eyes grew wide, and I put a finger to my lips, then crossed to her quickly, knelt and put my hand on her cheek. She kept her silence, eyes welling with tears. I put a finger to my lips again.

Then Marty yelled, "Police, hold it." I dashed to the doorway; a gunshot exploded, then another of a different caliber, and then three more, and I heard Marty yell "FUCK!" Turning into the corridor, I saw Marty's prone legs sticking out of the doorway, and when I got to him, blood was pouring from him and he was scrambling on his belly trying to reach his gun on the floor.

I was in the room now, Akibu standing in the middle pointing a .45 Colt automatic at Marty, repeatedly jerking at the trigger. A spent cartridge was sticking up from the pistol's ejection port, a smokestack jam. Easy enough to clear by brushing away the cartridge and pulling the slide back.

But Akibu didn't seem to know that.

I raised the Walther and aimed at the middle of his chest, and in that instant our eyes locked together. He threw his gun to the floor and raised his hands.

"This motherfucker *shot* me," Marty shouted, rolling onto his back.

I went to Marty, holding the gun on Akibu. "How bad is it?" I knelt to get a look at the wound. He'd been hit in the thigh, his pant leg darkened with blood.

Akibu actually looked amused.

"Fuck," Marty said. "Fuck, fuck, FUCK! I'm supposed to fucking *retire* next year." He propped himself up against the doorframe, and sat squeezing his thigh with both hands.

I dialed 911 on my cell phone, told the dispatcher we had a police officer shot and gave him the location.

"How you doing, Marty?" I said, eyes on Akibu, statue-still with his hands raised. Still smirking.

"I guess I'll make it. I just really, really wish I could have killed this motherfucker."

Now for the first time, Akibu spoke. He grinned at me. "Aren't you supposed to read me my rights now, Mistah Duncavan?"

I shook my head. "Uh-uh. I'm not the police. If I kill you now, you can't even call it police brutality."

His laugh was full of derision. Utterly confident, he said, "Listen to me, Mistah Duncavan." It was that same mesmerizing tone I'd heard over the phone. "Listen to my voice. Do you know how I come into your head? Why don't you put down the gun, now? It would be much better for you."

"I think it's time for you to shut up," I said.

"Why, will you shoot me?" Now he gave that big, rumbling laugh. "No, do not pretend to be my equal. You could not shoot down an unarmed man. I'm afraid it is your weakness."

I moved real close, looked him in the eye. He gave me a patronizing smile. "You shot my partner," I said.

That laugh again. "I know you, my Christian friend, I know you went to seminary for a time. Schooled by the Jesuits, wasn't it? No, you will not shoot me. Why don't you just lay your gun down, now? We can talk, then."

"Do you remember Butler?" I asked.

"Mike, don't do it," Marty said.

Akibu's eyes betrayed a flicker of uncertainty. He moved

them off mine for a second; then he looked at me sideways and gave a soft laugh. "No, Mistah Duncavan, I'm sorry, I don't know your Mr. Butler."

"Mike, no," Marty said.

"Wrong answer," I said, raised the pistol and shot him once in the chest. The bullet rocked him backward only slightly. He didn't even lower his arms, just lowered his astonished eyes to his chest, then raised them into mine.

I put the muzzle an inch from his chest and shot him twice more. He fell like a sack of pig feed then, and from the way his legs were twisted as he lay there, I knew he was dead when he hit the floor.

"Mike, Jesus Christ!"

"I thought that's what you wanted."

"You just can't go around shooting people."

"So, fucking arrest me." I knelt next to him again. "Just keep squeezing it. Keep the pressure on." There was a lot of blood, but I could see that the femoral artery was not hit.

I looked around the room, completely bare except for the table and a roll-top desk near where Marty sat against the wall. I went to the desk, started ripping drawers open, dumping the contents on the floor, happy to hear sirens wailing in the distance now.

"The fuck you looking for?" Marty said.

"A condom," I said.

"A condom," he repeated.

"A *used* condom."

"Oh," he said. "Well, call me extravagant, but I usually just throw them away."

I spilled out the top right drawer, then, and a zip-lock bag plopped onto the floor among the stick pens and index cards and paper clips. Inside was the condom.

"Mind picking that up for me?" I asked.

"I don't think so," Marty said.

"Well, I'll leave it for the evidence technician. I just hope they take good care of it. You got a handcuff key? I'd like to free the kid."

"What do you think I'd do with handcuffs? I'm a fucking *watch commander!*"

"I'm getting the feeling you're pissed at me for something," I said, and went out the door before he could answer.

In the next room, Lawanda's huge eyes stared wordlessly as I approached her, and I noticed for the first time how her face was drawn, her arms like sticks. God knows when she last had a meal. "Everything's going to be okay," I said. "Soon as somebody gets up here with a key, we'll get those things off you."

Then something that had been tugging at the back of my consciousness came to the fore: a strong odor. For just an instant I thought maybe it was because the kid hadn't had a bath in a while, but that wasn't it. It was more like a zoo smell. I looked around the room and spotted it then, the dog kennel at the other end, directly under the window where I couldn't see it from the roof across the street. I went over and I peeked in.

The hyena's corrugated flanks looked as though patches of fur had been torn away. But the animal ignored me. I seemed to be blocking his view. He swung his head impatiently from side to side, to get a look at Lawanda. As though anticipating that she would soon be carrion.

I went back to her, hunkered down and stroked her hair. "Hey, you know what? In just a little while, you're going to see your Mama." I put an arm around her shoulders and drew her to my chest. She squeezed her big eyes shut. Then her whole body shuddered, and erupted in deep, silent sobs.

CHAPTER FORTY-TWO

They took Marty and Lawanda to the hospital in the same ambulance. I wanted to ride along, but the paramedics said there wasn't room.

The sergeant in charge at the scene told me to stick around until the detectives got there, but I thought Marty and I ought to get the sequence of events straight first. As soon as I was sure the condom was in safe hands, I handed the sergeant my card, told him I'd be happy to give them a statement some other time, but I had to get over to the hospital. He actually told me I wasn't free to leave yet.

"You mean I'm under arrest?"

"No," he said.

"Then sayonara," I said. I thought they might try to stop me, but they didn't. I guess I wasn't exactly a flight risk.

I drove to Presbyterian St. Luke's, told the emergency room nurse that Lieutenant Richter was my partner. She led me back to a cubicle where Marty was stretched out on a gurney. His pant leg had been cut off, and his leg was swathed in a fat dressing. "They said it's superficial, through-and-through," he said, his head resting on an arm. "I'm probably going home."

"Did anyone call Donna?" I asked.

"No, I don't want anyone calling her from the hospital. If I'm going home, I'm going home. We probably ought to get straight what happened, though, before the dicks start taking statements."

"I had the same idea," I said.

"It's pretty simple. When I got to the doorway, the light in the room was poor and I didn't see anyone in there at first. Then, when I spotted this Akibu guy off in a corner, I yelled 'Police,' and he spun around with the .45 and fired several shots and hit me in the leg. Then you came running in and he pointed the gun at you, and you told him to drop it."

"That's the way I remember it."

"But he shot at you and you fired three times because he didn't fall down right away on account of you were using that pissy little .32 Walther, and he kept pointing the gun at you."

"Right."

"You had approached pretty close to him when you told him to drop it, because you didn't want to have to shoot the dirt bag and you thought maybe you could grab the gun away from him. That's how he got powder residue on his pretty red robes." His eyes drifted away. "Fuck," he said.

"What's the matter?"

"Nothing. It hurts."

Just then I sensed that someone was listening outside, and I raised a finger to my lips and tipped my head toward the curtain. Then the curtain moved aside and Detective Swain walked in with his clipboard.

"Funny," he said, looking at me. "I wonder how the African guy managed to shoot at you with this sticking out of the fucking ejection port." He held a zip-lock bag aloft with two fingers, a single spent .45 casing inside. Then with priestly ceremony he moved it to three points, first above Marty's head, then above mine, then above the plastic wastebasket. He dropped it in.

"The world is full of mysteries," he said. "This is a cleared case and I don't need a lot of extra paperwork. Lieutenant, let me know when you feel like giving a statement." Now he turned to me, chewing his gum as though he was afraid it might escape. "The patrol officers said you refused to wait for me at the scene. I know you don't like being told what to do, Duncavan, but I suggest you hang around here. I want to take statements while the two of you are together, 'cause I don't want to do this twice. As I said, I don't need a lot of extra paperwork. Get my drift?"

Subtle as Swain was, I got his drift, and was grateful. "I'll be here," I said.

Marty looked over at me and said, "Maybe you better call Donna, then."

Right after I called Donna, I called Beth to give her the good news—that it might take a few days of red tape, but Justin Ambertoe was virtually a free man.

But a man answered the phone.

"Who's this?" I asked.

"Who's *this?*" he responded, his words oozing testosterone.

"May I speak to Beth, please?" I was hoping that I'd misdialed, reached a wrong number. Hoping he'd say, "There's no Beth here."

But he didn't. When Beth came on, she seemed a little distant, though after I told her everything that happened, she erupted with joy. "Mike," she said, "this is such wonderful news!"

But then, she didn't say anything else.

"Who's the guy that answered the phone?" I asked. Like I was just making conversation.

"None of your business," she said, her tone equally conversational. Then she said, "Thanks so much for calling. Goodbye, Mike."

On the following morning, jury selection was supposed

to continue in Justin Ambertoe's trial, but instead Blake Canavan moved to continue the trial for one week, telling the judge there might be a voluntary dismissal. Normally a judge would not be kindly disposed to such judicial ineffi- ciency, but he'd read the morning papers and surely under- stood. He granted the continuance but on his own motion declared a mistrial, dismissed the jurors and told the attor- neys he'd see them next week.

In the days that followed, the police determined that the unknown fingerprint on Reggie Brockton's scooter was in- deed Dwani Mwenyako's, aka David Akibu. And testing de- termined that Justin Ambertoe's DNA matched the semen found in the condom recovered from Akibu's desk drawer.

I gave the police the address of Clyde Temple's parents, and a warrant was issued for his arrest. If he was still alive, sooner or later I knew he'd be picked up on the warrant—probably sooner, since he was the kind of guy the police noticed.

I went over to the court on the day Justin's trial was to re- sume and sat in the back. I thought Justin would be there, but he wasn't. When the judge came on the bench, Stan Janda and Blake Canavan rose from the counsel tables and approached, and Blake made a formal motion to drop all charges.

The caged hyena we'd found in the building was accepted by the Brookfield Zoo. I went to see it once, in the outdoor African mammals exhibit where it had space to roam, its coat looking much healthier, its ribs no longer prominent. It paced nervously the whole time I sat there, shifting suspi- cious eyes in every direction, but especially, it seemed, at me.

The other hyena, the one I'd seen in the park, was never seen again. At least not that I know of. Maybe it's still there, wedged between two worlds, trying to earn its living in the night.

255

ABOUT THE AUTHOR

A Chicago native, THOMAS J. KEEVERS is a trial lawyer and former homicide detective with the Chicago Police Department. His first novel in the Mike Duncavan series, *Music Across the Wall*, was published by Five Star Publishing in December, 2003. Keevers' short stories have appeared in *The Chicago Literary Review Quarterly*, *Wind Magazine*, *Innesfree* and *The Clockwatch Review*. His short-short, "Thanksgiving Day in Homicide," was anthologized in *New Chicago Stories*, and later featured on National Public Radio's "Stories on Stage." For more, see www.thomaskeevers.com.